TAVEN'S DEPARTING

MIKE JACKSON

DEDICATION

To my wife, who is more than I could have dreamt her to be. To my children, who bring real purpose to my life. To my parents, who are everything parents ought to be and more.

CONTENTS

ACKNOWLEDGMENTS

Many thanks to everyone who read this book at various stages and for their very important input. I wouldn't have got here without your help.

Prologue

She screams against her will. Unbound but rooted to the spot, she gasps. Slowly straightening she readies herself for the next blow. The merciless whip crosses her back and grazes her cheek, leaving a glowing red mark that fades leaving no evidence of the violence done to her. Another blow wrenches her breath from her. She staggers forward. Before she can inhale, the crack of the whip resonates in the space in which only the two of them are visible.

Now on her knees, her limbs no longer respond to her will. "I... please..."

The faceless humanoid, created only for the purpose of torture, draws his arm back and sends her sprawling with the force of the swing.

"What do you think you are?" The question does not come from the torturer, but enters the void as the voice of raging fire. "You are a fool. You are weak. You are worthless."

The woman's voice creaks, "I have nothing to give to you. I can't give you what you want."

The torturer's boot strikes below her armpit.

"You can't or you won't?" growled the bodiless voice.

"I can't... I can't..." she sobs. The torturer strikes her across her stomach. She flails.

"If you can't, then find someone who can."

"Please. I'll do anything." A foot is driven into her ribs. She tenses too late. She wasn't ready. "Who do you want?"

"Look." The torturer now has a face. Although she's never seen the man before, he is familiar.

"I won't fail you." She cringes. The arm is raised to strike again. "I won't."

The nothingness folds in on itself, taking with it the faceless being and the voice. In an instant, she's back in the room large enough only for her to stand. Metallic. Cold. She turns and pushes through the tangible dark haze that is the exit. The subterranean cavern, hewn by nature's steady and unrelenting persuasion, lined by entrances like the one she's exited, looms before her. A man stands near the center. She approaches him. Nothing said. Her hand on his shoulder, the room vanishes from their view.

"Why did you bother resisting?" the man asks her as a field materializes around them. "As soon as we brought you here, you became one of us."

She grabs the back of his arm. He pulls it away as though he's been electrified.

"Stop it," he yells. "Don't touch me like that again or I'll kill you."

The woman looks to the ground then back at the grimacing man. "Haven't you already?"

Waking up

I am... I am... Taven.

Consciousness dawned. A being stood before me. She was instantly familiar, but like words aching to leap off the tongue and slipping and sinking into the saliva, her face, her body, her voice were veiled, muffled and soon lost to me.

The darkness that was her canvass burst into swirling colors. My eyes darted from one point to another, trying to make sense of what was in front of me but the brightness overwhelmed my ability to comprehend. I had to close my eyes. Greens and blues continued to swirl around the inside of my head. It was like I was being drawn into another place. The blue settled on the top half, lighter shades of blue above the horizontal line, green below.

Understanding slowly distilled. I recognized a field that looked like it was covered in carpet. But it had to be grass because carpet is inside. Somehow I knew what carpet was and what grass was.

I opened my eyes.

Blurred rings surrounded everything I could see, the horizon line of the land and sky, the melded lump of leaves on the trees, a grey streak not far from me crossed the green grass on which I sat. This wasn't in my mind. I was experiencing outside of self, experiencing something other. I blinked. My focus improved but remained visually off, like watching a videocassette after experiencing high definition.

I looked down. My hand looked no different than I somehow knew it had looked before, whenever or whatever before was. That there was a before was as certain for me as existence, but I could not lay hold on any of its details. No blemishes; my nails were perfectly trimmed, no scar from when my hand was slammed in the car door.

The memory of the experience faded before I could grasp it. It was almost as though I had never even remembered it.

My fingers moved at my command but I couldn't feel the blades of the grass I sat in, or the friction between my fingers. I opened and closed my hand. There was no tingle in my fingertips, no creak in the wrist, no pull of the ligaments.

Understanding attempted to make its appearance, but I blocked it. I wasn't ready for it.

I recognized the sounds I would have expected to exist in a place like this, except I didn't really hear them, I just knew them, like when I used to replay a song I really liked in my own head.

I inhaled, but felt nothing: no brush against my nostrils, no rush into my lungs, no relief. I didn't need to breathe. I had never appreciated it, but there was something calming about the rhythmic and constant experience of breathing.

I looked down and saw what looked like my body. I had on my favorite pair of jeans, the ones that were just baggy enough that I could play a pick-up game of basketball without having to go home to change first but nice enough that it didn't look like I'd just played basketball in them.

I had on the t-shirt I wore the night Eve danced with me at the school dance.

"Who's Eve?" It was my voice but it was effortlessly produced. The embers of the memory were all that remained.

Socks on, running shoes on my feet, I was dressed the way I did when I was alive. When I was alive. "I'm dead."

I was alone in the field. I would have given anything to speak to anyone at that moment to confirm that conclusion. My mind stuttered through the many pieces of information, grasping for anything that would provide a bearing, never able to seize upon something that rose above doubt.

"Is there anyone here?"

I stared at a tree in the distance, allowing my vision to blur as I delved inside myself, looking for answers, for reasons. Just before the point of blackness, it was like I had turned on a switch, restoring the vibrancy of color and perfection of focus to my eyes. The rising sun came suddenly into view, casting a pink and purple hue over the string of clouds clinging to the horizon. What was little more than a painter's concept of grass, trees and sky was now the real thing. A path ran directly through the field in which I stood, dividing me from a swing set and a slide, which I now saw on the other side of it. A determined female jogger ran up the path towards me.

"Where am I?" I asked.

Although she stared in my general direction, she did not answer.

"Hey, lady." I stepped into the middle of the path. "Am I dead?"

The woman, dressed in a turquoise tracksuit with white stripes up the side, continued at a steady pace toward me as though she hadn't seen me.

"Can you hear me?" I asked again. I stood my ground for a while but right before she would have collided with me, I stepped out of the way. She ran past me without the slightest acknowledgment.

"Wait!" I reached for her arm. Other than the memory of the feel of the polyester material, I felt nothing and she continued to swing her arm as though I wasn't there.

Unwilling to give up yet, I rationalized it was because of the earphones she was unable to hear what I had said. I placed my fingers around the earphone cord and tugged. My fingers slid down the cord. I tried to grab the cord but my fingers wouldn't fit in the space between her neck and the plastic casing and I couldn't force them to. I waited until the cord bunched up and slid my fingers through. No sooner had I grasped it, it tightened again, pinching my fingers. I jerked my hand free before they could be severed.

She continued down the path as though I didn't exist. Maybe I didn't for her.

Not wanting to be left alone, I followed the woman along the asphalt walkway, although not at her pace. We left the clearing and passed to a shaded portion of the path. Tall evergreen and deciduous trees lined the sides.

Not long after I'd begun following her, the veil of trees on one side opened to a plain view of the waterway that ran alongside the path. Captivated by the soft ripple and glistening sun on the surface of the slow moving water, I abandoned my pursuit of the anonymous female jogger.

Crouching by the water's edge, I dipped my finger into the water and was disappointed to have nothing more than a memory of wetness. The water seemed to pass right through me because there was nothing in the behavior of the water to indicate my finger was in it.

I stood then walked into the river.

I was unaffected by the cold or the current. The water rose to my knees and quickly over my waist. I dove into the water. I might as well have been made of lead because I fell to the bed of the river. Flipping from my face to my back, I felt no pressure or movement, nor did I suffer from a lack of oxygen as I lay there.

The water streamed by. Flecks of material carried by the water sparkled in the sunlight. Even the slimy log, cradled by the river, had the same heavenly hue. A fish effortlessly glided downstream, then hovered immediately above me as if a sign that I was not completely unnoticed. I reached up. The fish did not respond to my movement. I imagined the sensation of touching the cold and slippery scales. My fingers halted on the side of the fish but I felt nothing but I couldn't resist the serpentine movements of the fish as it maintained its place in the current. As long as I touched the fish, my hand waived along with it. I stood up. The fish hovered in front of my chest, its tail towards me. Without warning, it turned and gave in to the current, easily pushing me out of the way, as though I had no more mass than one of the sparkling flecks in the water. Feeling as insignificant as my impact on the fish was, I walked out of the stream and back to the only familiar thing to me: the path.

Streams of people now trod it. I walked against the grain, back to the field where I began. Spread throughout the park, groups of people mingled, connected, laughed, interacted. I was unnoticed. A desperate loneliness gripped me beyond any experience available to me now.

A line of five children, all less than six years old, was at the long, curved, metal slide at the edge of the park. I approached a small girl with dark brown eyes, black pigtails and olive skin. She wore a frilly lavender dress and shiny black shoes. I hoped this girl would be able to see me; her innocence could pierce the veil separating us. I knelt next to her so we were eye level and I whispered, "Can you see me?"

"No," she responded.

My heart leapt but I didn't want to count this a victory before I was sure it was. I asked, "Can you hear me?"

"No," she said. "I'm not allowed to talk to you."

This was the first time, since I'd been dead, I felt like I was actually having an impact, like I was being heard. "What's your name?"

"Stop it," she shouted, her chubby face now darkened by her crinkled brow. I placed my hand on her shoulder.

"I know I'm dead but you don't have to be afraid of me. I'm a ghost, but not a scary one. A nice one. You know, like one who helps people and stuff. Did you know I..."

"Don't touch me," she growled, her arms now rigid.

I took my hand off her shoulder with surprise. "I'm sorry. I was so happy to have someone to..."

"Don't touch me," she said again.

"But I'm not touching you any more, see?" I said, waving my hands in front of her. "I won't do it again. I'm sorry."

"Stop it!" and with those two words the little girl turned and shoved the boy behind her, sending him to his backside. He immediately burst into tears. Two mothers raced from the benches where they had been watching the action. One of the mothers stepped right into me, pushing me out of the way. She knelt in the very spot I had been kneeling. "Why did you push that little boy?" she asked the little girl.

"He pinched my bum," said the little girl.

"No I didn't," I said simultaneously with the little boy lying on the ground, his overalls now covered in dust. The wide-eyed head-shaking solemnity of the little boy were an evidence of deception.

The second mother then asked the child that was apparently her son, "Frederick, what did I tell you about pinching other people's bums?"

"I don't know," he answered.

"Frederick Wilson Jacobson, you tell me the truth right now. I know you got hurt but you need to tell me," the mother said, as she hauled the little boy to his feet.

"I just... I just... I just poked a little with my finger right here," he said as he pointed to his own lower back.

"Frederick!"

Frederick looked at his feet. "You told me not to pinch people's bums."

"You say you're sorry," the second mother commanded.

"Sorry, girl."

"Gloria, I've told you about pushing. You tell me if you've got a problem, okay? Now you go say you're sorry," the first mother said to the little girl.

"Sorry, boy," Gloria said to Frederick.

"Frederick is his name," Gloria's mother corrected.

"But he called me girl."

"Gloria."

"Sorry... Frederick," Gloria snarled.

"That's okay..." Frederick paused until the mothers turned from them. "Girl."

The conflict had cleared the line up to the slide, so I climbed the ladder and went down. No squeak as I descended, no wind in my face, no drop in my stomach, no risk of physical harm. Needless to say it wasn't much of an experience.

I sat on the ground at the bottom of the slide, pondering. Before I could come to any conclusions, Frederick came down the slide, planted both feet in my back and sent me out of the way and onto my face. He unknowingly kicked me along, log-like in front of him. The only option was to leap out of the way, which I eventually did.

"If I could haunt you, I would," I said. I didn't really mean it; at least I don't think I did.

I left the slide and walked to the middle of the field. A large man, with a long gait and a big dog, walked the path that crossed the field. He threw a chewed up tennis ball right at me. I caught the ball but was carried by its momentum until it came to a stop, pinning me to the ground. The dog charged and having stepped on me, tore the ball from my grip, as if I wasn't there and continued on its way.

I dusted myself off, although there was no dust to be dusted, and walked over to a nearby poplar tree. I needed a safe place to process what was happening. I sat down under it. The dog, ball clamped in its jaws, made its way directly for me. It stopped and sniffed at the area around me. "Can you smell me, boy? If you can, I guess that's better than nothing at all." I placed my hands on the dog's side and scratched, unable to change the lie of its hair.

Without warning, the dog spun sideways and relieved himself. The yellow stream passed right through me. He finished, back-kicked grass in my direction, and then trotted back to his master.

Not eating

I sat at a tree near the tree where the dog had staked his claim for a long time. Gloria was still at the slide shoving every boy who stood in line behind her, whether or not they actually touched her, bicycles rode down the path in an interminable chain, not one of them looking at me, and groups of people of every sort gathered for picnics at the dozens of picnic tables scattered throughout the park. At one of the tables, not more than an eight year old's stone throw from me, sat what seemed to me to be a family; similar faces distinguished mainly by hair color and the presence, or absence, of wrinkles. I didn't feel hungry, but when I saw the hamburgers, the hot dogs, the cans of pop, the chips spread out across the table, I craved them.

A woman had torn up a dripping with juices, perfectly cooked, hamburger for a young child, apparently old enough to eat solid food. Having clawed at the chunks of meat on the plastic plate on the table with the precision of a crane from a cord grappling hook prize game, the infant clumsily jammed the sumptuous meat into her mouth. As the child gummed the meat, she only had fangs no molars that I could see, there was no evidence of appreciation on her face for the delicious morsel.

It was all I could take. I approached the table and sat next to a silver-haired woman, who mirrored, literally and figuratively, the younger woman that was feeding the infant, placing me next to the child opposite the woman feeding her, which I assumed was her mother.

"Are you ready for another bite?" the younger woman asked.

The child shook her head violently with her mouth clamped shut.

"If she won't eat it I will," I said, to no response at all. Being that no one opposed me, I leaned toward the plate and chose the smallest possible piece. "I just need to concentrate."

I attempted to pick it up and failed no matter how much I strained, flexed or grunted. It wasn't that it was too heavy, and it wasn't slippery but it acted like it was too slippery to pick up. I couldn't grip it.

"Come on, Jessica. Be a good girl. Open your mouth. Like this." The woman's mouth gaped open. It looked like her eyebrows were being pulled to her hairline. Any closer and they might have leapt right off her head.

I looked both ways and lowered my head to the shredded beef I'd been trying to pick up and licked it. I don't know what was more disappointing; the fact that there was no salty thrill, no juiciness, no invigoration, no taste on putting my tongue to the meat or the fact that I'd just tried to lick a baby's food but that disappointment did not discourage me from trying again. The draw of the food was stronger than my disgust.

I positioned my head between her hand and her face. I opened my mouth. She mashed a bit of meat in her hand and lifted it, inserting her hand into my mouth. "Just let it go," I said not moving my jaw.

Unaware of me, she pressed on and as she did, my head involuntarily titled. Her hand slid along the roof of my mouth, over my teeth, which folded over to allow her to pass, past my lips, where she flattened my nose as she inserted the morsel into her mouth. She threw both arms into the air to celebrate her triumph. As I sat on the ground next to the girl, I appreciated perfectly her sense of achievement and my detachment from the world that was so familiar and yet unreachable.

I closed my eyes.

Immediately I was hanging over my mother and my five-year-old self in our kitchen. The table where we ate supper, which was situated in what some families might use as a breakfast nook, was separated from the stove, the sink, the microwave and the fridge by a row of overhanging wooden cupboards and a counter that was about the same height as I was at that time. Mom stood next to the kitchen sink washing dishes. I sat alone at the table, my plate full of food. On the other side of the table, and down two steps was the living room, where my baby sister played with my father.

"Taven. You will sit at this table until you eat your beans. Do you understand me?" my mother said, in a voice of strained patience.

"But I hate them. They're so gross. I'm not going to eat them," the younger version of me whined, as he distastefully poked at the beans.

"You are going to eat them," Mom began, the patient façade now gone, and rage emerging, "I am not your slave and if you think you can pick and choose what you're going to eat in this house, you are mistaken. If you think any child of mine is going to be so picky that he won't eat what's put in front of him, you are wrong. You will be eating this food, if you have to sit here until your bedtime."

I had never really enjoyed beans, at least that's what I understood about myself, but in that instant I appreciated the beans, and the opportunity to eat them in a way I never had before. "Just eat them," I said to the five-year old version of myself. It was like yelling at the television during the big soccer game. The attempt would be futile but at least I felt like there was a chance I could change the outcome.

"I don't want to," the me at the table grumbled defiantly.

"Eat the beans," I pled.

My mother stomped around the cupboards to the plain view of little me. "Excuse me? I don't want to? So. I guess we all get to choose what we want and don't want to do. Well. I don't want to do the laundry. Attention everybody. Mom's not going to do laundry any more. Oh. I bet Dad doesn't want to go to work anymore. Attention everybody. We're going to have to live in a cardboard box and eat dirt because Dad doesn't want to work anymore." The little me was cringing at the tirade, but his hand was no closer to his fork. "It doesn't work that way, Taven. You are going to eat those beans."

My mother was now standing directly over the little me. I watched him resentfully pick up the fork and direct it towards his mouth. He stopped short and sobbed uncontrollably. "I'm going to throw up. It's too gross," the little me choked through his tears. He even threw in a gag.

My mother, normally a saintly woman, was now growling. "You will not be throwing up at the dinner table. If you can't do it yourself, I'll put it in your mouth. Open your mouth." The little me opened his mouth enough to allow the tip of a bean to enter.

Seizing the opportunity, my mother quickly shoved the fork into his mouth. And the gagging really began. "Don't you dare. Do you know how many children around the world have nothing to eat? Do not spit those out! That's what I told you not to do. I'm not helping you, nope, not going to do it," she said as she charged back to the sink. "Rather than sit here and eat those beans, you'd prefer to spit them out? Is that it?"

"Don't do it, come on, don't nod, no," I shouted.

Despite my efforts, which I knew where of little use any way, little me nodded his head.

"Did you just nod your head? John, did he just nod his head?" my mother asked.

"I'm not sure dear," said my father from the other room, sounding a little afraid he might bring on the wrath of Mom too if he wasn't careful about what he said.

"You did nod your head. I will not stand for that kind of disrespect," she said as she balled up the towel she was clinging to and threw it on the counter next to the sink. As she started to pull the apron off and was nearly around the cupboards, the five year old me finally realized what was at stake.

"I'll eat. I'll eat," he said.

"Then do it or I am going to come over there and it will not be to help you eat your beans," she said.

He slowly picked up the fork and poked the beans lightly, as though they might burst if he poked too hard.

"Taven, eat! Scoop up those beans and put them in your mouth."

He slowly moved the fork from the top of the mound of beans to the side, and slid the fork underneath.

"Now pick them up and put them in your mouth," she said.

His face contorted as though he were about to be forced to eat a dung sandwich. The fork inched towards little me's mouth, which opened as though his bottom jaw was being drawn open by tiny little work men pulling it down against his will. At last, the beans passed the threshold of the teeth.

In an instant I was drawn back to my present surroundings and the now empty table at which the baby once sat. "What did that have to do with anything?" I asked the midnight sky.

Although there was no answer, I understood, I knew, it was a memory. As silly as it seemed, it gave me bearings. In some other existence, I had parents. I had a home.

My trip downtown

It took my a while to push away the irritation that kept creeping in. Of all of the memories to remind me of my origins, the *me not eating my beans* memory was not a natural boost to my ego. It was hard not to take it personally. The only clear memory of my mother and my father were at that dinner where I acted like a spoiled brat. I battled the doubts of whether it was a message of my worth and value, or of the absurdity of my existence. But as the night wore on, a gratitude for what I now had, regardless of how I got it, joined the hurt and the uncertainty. At least I had something to move forward with. At least I had a hint of where I came from.

Standing once again, I walked to the path and followed it beyond the point where I had jumped into the river and continued walking as the sun rose, its rays casting a pinkish glow to clouds visible over the tops of the trees, the many shades of blue in the once dark sky now apparent. As I walked on, more and more people joined me on the path, many of whom were not dressed in the workout tops and shorts but rather in what seemed to me to be trendy business attire and shiny shoes, some with rounded ends, others pointed, the click clack click clack accompanying me as I walked along with this growing throng.

After walking for what seemed a long time, the trees gave way to a large bridge which passed over a busy highway running from east to west and from west to east, cars, trucks, vans, motorcycles, buses and other vehicles careening along it, the bridge leading to what were dozens of tall buildings reaching up to the sky.

I allowed myself to be guided by the crowd to the very heart of downtown and to the rush of people arriving on foot, by train, by bike, by bus and by car. After passing several busy roads, I stopped at a street where road traffic had been completely cut off and hundreds or maybe thousands of people on foot, most dressed better than I, flowed past me.

I moved over to the sidewalk and sat on a steel-framed bench with wooden slats for a seat, marveling at the way people streamed past as though they were a watercourse, the collective group following the path of least resistance.

"If we don't get that order out by this afternoon, it'll be the end of him," a pudgy bald man said, walking with a faster pace than his girth would suggest possible.

"Last night was awesome. Did you see the way Samantha was all over me? Left her lying there in my apartment this morning," boasted a guy in what appeared to be his early twenties, with slicked back black hair, grey pin-striped suit, tailed by four other men similarly dressed.

"You're gross," I shouted. It seemed for a moment that the four trailing men scowled in my direction, but I knew that was in my head. I don't know why, but I knew it was wrong to treat a person more like a plaything to be used than a human being.

"This daycare is way better than the last one so I'm sure she'll get used to it," said one well-coiffed mature woman to another to the rhythm of their heels.

"Your arguments fly in the face of precedent. Justice Freeborn will see right through your ..." a woman wearing what looked like evening apparel snapped at a man dressed in long black robes with a white collar.

"None of it matters!" I shouted at the crowd, suddenly filled with a rage that prickled through me. It was as though I was no longer myself, or rather, my anger became me. "You're wasting your time. Before you know it you'll be like me. Nothing you do will make a bit of difference."

"You got that right, buddy," said a voice. A grizzled old man appeared from the crowd and walked toward me. Dressed to match everyone else, a week's worth of stubble adorned his jaw and dark circles seemed painted under his hungry and haggard eyes.

"You can hear me?" I asked him.

"Did you think you were the only dead person here?" he asked, as he laughed at me. I laughed along with him but it didn't change the fact that I knew he was laughing at me.

"What's your name?" I asked.

"Who cares? Whatever it was, it doesn't mean anything any way. I just exist and I can't stop," he said sitting next to me on the bench.

"What are you doing here?" I inched away from him. His negative essence was like a rancid smell and seemed to increase the intensity of what I was experiencing.

"Same thing you're doing here. Nothing. Can't do a thing. Next best thing is seeing someone else enjoying what I used to. Cruel trick. When I threw myself out of the building over there, I figured it was the end. And I wanted it to be," he said, as though he were talking about what he had had for breakfast. He pointed with his thumb to a tall building that acted like a gigantic mirror, reflecting the image of the other buildings around it, owing to the windows that reached from the ground to the top.

"You killed yourself?" I asked.

"You would have too... in my place. I lost everything. One bad move on what should have been a sure thing. How was I supposed to know the financial statements were fraudulent and management was crooks. In my heyday, I managed a multi-billion dollar fund. One bad move, one swing in the markets and I'm out of a job and they're threatening to sue me," he said, his voice steady but accompanied by a tangible hatred.

"I'm sorry..." I stammered, but he continued as though I'd not spoken.

"My wife left me. Couldn't blame her, we hardly knew each other anymore. I was too busy to miss her and when I wasn't busy I was trying to manage the built up stress. At the office fifteen hours a day, when I didn't sleep there, and when I wasn't at the office, I was out drinking or cheating. I thought I was having fun, but it was pain management. When I lost my job she stuck with me, at first. But when she caught me with another woman, she left me. It wasn't until she was gone that I realized how much that tie with her meant. But it was too late. When the company sued me..."

"How could they sue you if you didn't do anything wrong?" I asked, conflicted as to whether I felt sorry for this man or not.

"Kid, the only way you make it here," the man pointed the index fingers on both hands making the shapes of guns towards the buildings on opposite sides of the street, "is by doing anything it takes. There's no right. There's no wrong. There's only getting caught and not getting caught. People cheat by following rules and people cheat by breaking them. I was one of the unlucky ones that got caught while breaking them and it's not like I was the only one doing it. I wasn't really hurting anybody. Only reason people got hurt was because we got caught. If we wouldn't have been caught, everyone would be blissfully unaware and rich because of what we were doing."

"So why did you, you know..." I asked, propelled in my question by morbid curiosity.

"Kill myself? Because my run was over. I couldn't get any of the things I wanted any more. The divorce cost me my house and my cars. The lawsuit cost me my reputation and whatever money I had left. I wasn't going to live on the street like some beggar. I was better than that. I came to the conclusion that it would be better to not exist, than to not have the things I wanted most. That's why this is hell. I can't have any of the things I want and when I close my eyes all I see is me using the old key I never gave back, sneaking into the stairwell, climbing the stairs, smug and confident, glad I would be taking back control, through the door to the building's roof and with only enough hesitation to curse whatever gods there might be, I jumped. And then I see the small child, who watched the whole thing." He looked like he was describing what was then present before him. He shook his head. "She saw what I did. And almost more than the pain I caused myself, the pain I caused her haunts me. An innocent little girl tainted. I don't care. I hate her, but I can't shake the remorse. I found her later, but was tormented all the more."

"Why?" I asked.

"Because I couldn't help but blame myself for everything that went wrong in her life. I set her down the wrong course. I hate her and I hate myself," he shouted at me.

Despite being horrified, chilled to the bone by his story, curiosity drove me to ask what I thought I needed. "How did you find the girl? Can you tell me how you did it?"

"Why would I help you? I hate you and I hate everything that's here. I'm not going to help you," he shouted, as he stood and pointed his finger in my face.

"What did I do to you?" I asked, conflicted about him backing away from me.

"Nothing. Why would I help you get what you want, when I've got nothing that I want?" Without waiting for an answer, he turned away and melted into the flow of people.

I wondered what I had done to deserve being abandoned to a place where I couldn't have anything that I wanted and a man like that was. How did I die? Was I a murderer? I couldn't be. I knew that wasn't who I was. The anger inside me faded with that thought.

Anxious to get out of a place that had been witness to such horrific things, I crossed the road and, cutting across the flow of people, I made my way to the next street over, which was far less busy. Not far from me, a group of people huddled next to the side of a building. I walked over feeling much more timid after this first experience.

"What are you doing?" I asked, not sure whether I was speaking to the living or the dead.

Since no one answered, I attempted to slip between a man and a woman to get a better look at what was in the middle of the group.

"Back off. I was here first," the woman snapped.

"Sorry. I didn't realize you were dead," I said, stepping away from the circle.

"Great. A funny guy. Thanks for reminding me. Go find yourself another smoker, 'kay?" she growled at me.

"Another smoker?" I asked.

"Leave me alone. I don't want to miss this. I'm done with you," she shouted.

I turned back towards the road, and noticed something I hadn't on the busier street I first found myself on. A person, wearing a hoody and ragged jeans, one of the few casually dressed people around, rushed down the street, cigarette in hand, surrounded by other people who were not smoking, but were clearly interested in the person smoking. Every time the cigarette went to the lips, the heads of the crowd leaned in, an audible communal moan accompanying each puff, which I assumed was their disappointment in not being able to take the smoke themselves. I thought back to the young man who boasted about sleeping with Samantha, the poor girl who had clearly made a terrible mistake, and remembered that he was talking into a cellphone, and wondered whether the men following him were alive.

"Get away from me!" The same woman shrieked. Before I could turn around, a tingling in my back sent me stumbling forward into the middle of the road and into the path of a rusty, muddy four-by-four truck. In an instant, my torso folded over the grill of the truck causing my face to strike the hood. I felt no pain, but I also had no control over my circumstances. I thought I heard laughing, but I lost the sound as I was sent up and over the windshield and into the air, landing in front of a mall entrance. I turned, expecting the woman's derisive finger to be in my direction, but I could not see her. She was likely buried in the crowd of people starving for the aroma of cigarettes.

Despite sitting on a sensor that would have opened the door, the door remained shut. It wasn't until someone walked close enough to the door that I was able to leave the scene of my embarrassment.

The mall entrance opened to a broad hallway, flanked by stores selling men's apparel, woman's footwear, knives and specialty popcorn, and was filled with people rushing busily to and fro, seeming to care little about anything but their destination. Square ceramic tiles lined the floor. The ceiling resembled the inside of a warehouse. The clicking of the fancy shoes on the floor did not keep the beat of the music playing in the background that spoke of a different era.

"Hey, you. Kid. Come over here."

I didn't see who had said it, but it came from a group of men huddled in front of the woman's footwear store. "Me?"

"No, the other dead guy standing in the entrance," said the raspy voice. The sound of mirthless and mocking laughter followed.

I looked around.

"You ain't too bright, are ya kid? Come over here. You might be good for a few laughs."

I was hesitant to approach another group, but at least these people seemed interested in me. "Hi, I'm Taven."

"What kind of name is that?" said a gruff voice, quickly followed by a "Who cares?" that was almost drowned out in the same laughing at my expense.

"If you guys are just going to laugh at me, I'll be on my way."

The crowd parted. A heavily-stubbled, balding man, dressed in a florescent shirt and shorts, an upside down visor on his head, said, "Did he just say he was going to leave, Julius?"

"Uh huh." The large man nodded.

"Just who does he think he is?" The visored-man scanned his group and then answered his own question. "Oh right, it's Ta-veen. Look, Ta-veen. When I talk to you, you better listen. You ain't got nothin' more important to do than what I'm tellin' you you gotta do. Got it?"

As much as I didn't want to admit it, he was right. I didn't have anything more important to do because I had no idea what to do. "What are you guys doing?"

"Just wait and see. You watch this time and we'll let you join in the next time around," At that moment, a distinguished looking woman with an animal fur shawl, tan blouse, leather knee length skirt, brown tights, leather heeled boots, and two large bags, presumably filled with newly purchased shoes, turned away from the till and towards the store's entrance.

"She's going to the bathroom down the third corridor," a deep voice called from the other side of the crowd.

"Dress shop down the way," a scratchy older sounding voice called out.

"Coffee shop on Main Street and Third Avenue," another called.

"She's getting a manicure on the second floor," another called.

"She's going to work," a skinny man shouted.

"Tony. How many times I gotta tell you that's not good enough? It's too general. Your vote don't count," said the man with the visor.

The skinny man tried again, "how about the stock exchange tower on Fifth Avenue."

The man with the visor pointed right at Tony. "Too late." The group bounced out of the way of the woman as she passed through.

"You and you," the visored-man said pointing at me and another man. "Follow her."

"I don't even know what you're doing. Why should I have to go?"

"Why? Why? I'll tell you why. 'Cause I told you to," the visored-man responded.

Threats from a dead guy did not worry me. I'd spent hours in freezing cold river water and had been hit by a truck. "What are you going to do? Kill me?" I looked around, half expecting the crowd to join in with the same mocking laughter as before but it seemed like everyone had taken a step away from me.

"I'll deal with this guy in a second. Tony, you go instead. If you screw this up I'll really show you the meaning of too late." Without responding the two appointed men rushed after the woman.

I turned to the man named Julius, who stood next to me, and whispered, "What are you guys doing?"

He whispered, "I don't want Elmer to see me talking to you 'cause then he ain't gonna tell me his secret. But if it will shut you up, and I mean I want you to shut up" he paused to wait for Elmer to reengage in another conversation "I'll tell you." He waited for me to nod. "We're gambling on where the shoppers are going next."

"And what do you win if you get it right?" I asked.

"I told you to shut up. You ain't gonna win a thing by the time Elmer's done with you."

"What's the secret?" I asked.

"What about shut up do you not understand?"

"I'm dead. What difference does it make?"

"You're gonna find out real soon Ta-veen." Elmer had left his conversation and was now standing within an arm's length of Julius and I.

"Umm, I'm actually not that interested. Good luck with guessing where the lady is going for no apparent reason," I said as I turned to walk away.

Elmer walked around to stand right in front of me, his visor nearly touching the bridge of my nose. "I ain't done with you."

"Yes you are. And what are you going to do? Not tell me your secret?"

Elmer fired a glance at Julius. "Julius. When are you going to learn to shut up?"

"It was the kid's fault. He wouldn't leave me alone."

"I'll let you off this time. Grab Ta-veen for me. We don't want him to run away on us." The group took hold of my arms and legs. I didn't feel their hands but I couldn't move.

"You ready?" Elmer asked me.

"For what?" I responded.

He slowly drove his fist into my stomach. Pain erupted in my belly, not physical pain, although it was like it, but negative energy coursed through every inch of me like a million unfixable regrets. Hurting, helpless and hopeless, I crumpled to the ground. "That, Ta-veen, was just a love tap. Once Tony gets back, I'm gonna really show you my secret."

I stood. "I'm not sure you have anything worth me hearing. If it's all the same to you, I'm ready to leave."

He struck me across the face. The same sensation burnt my eyes and my cheek, only it lingered longer than the first time.

Instinctively I swung, my fist on a collision course with his jawbone. He didn't even flinch as I made contact. I felt nothing and apparently neither did he. "What was that? How dumb can you be? Ready to feel my secret again?" He drew his arm back to strike me again.

"Fancy lady went to the bathroom," the large man with the deep voice yelled as he jogged towards us. "I was right."

"Is he cheating?" Elmer asked Tony.

"No he's not cheating, she went to the bathroom on main street," Tony said.

"On Main Street, did she?" Elmer asked.

The deep-voiced man shot a deadly look at Tony. Tony stammered, "No, I mean the bathroom down the second corridor."

"There is no bathroom down the second corridor," said Elmer. He stood and stepped towards the two men. "Look if you guys want me to be nice, you gotta be nice. Cheating ain't nice. It wrecks the game. Cheaters ain't nothin' but an example. You wreck the game, I wreck you."

Elmer leapt at both of the messengers striking them savagely. The attention fully on those other two, I bolted for the exit. Closely tailing a man on his cellphone, I slipped out the door.

Pining for Eve

"Where do you think you're going?" It was Elmer. I don't know how he found me. As soon as I escaped the mall, I sprinted across the street angling my way back home, or at least the only place that was familiar enough to call home: my field. "I ain't finished with you."

It didn't matter how fast I ran, or where I hid, he was always next to me, mocking me. I ran down the middle of the street. I didn't care about the cars. They couldn't hurt me. He could. I turned my head to find him. By the time I looked back he was there.

"Not too smart, are you?" His fist collided with my jaw. Searing pain wracked my body. "You finished so quick?"

I punched him again, making direct contact with his cheek.

"Good try," he laughed as he dropped me to my knees with a kick to my ribs. Strike after strike, each point of contact an epicenter of suffering.

"What do you want from me?"

"I thought I couldn't do anything to you. I'm just making sure that I was right and you were wrong." He wound up to strike again but before he could a woman stood between us, facing him. That's when I lost all awareness of my surroundings and Eve flooded my mind.

She wasn't a cheerleader or with the *in* crowd, but everyone liked her. I think it was because she made everyone at the high school, well, at least the hundred and fifty boys, more or less, feel like her favorite. And I think many of us hoped we might be. She wasn't flirty or over the top in her appearance, she usually wore a hoodie and faded blue jeans, but she always said "hi", always had a smile on her face and was always interested in what you had to say.

I worked as a vendor to raise money for college. I used to park my vending cart at the baseball games, despite the rodeo being a more lucrative venue, hoping, just hoping, she would come when no one else was buying a hot dog so we could have our moment. While swimming in calm memory, I was caught in the tide of vivid experience. The ball diamond, hot dog cart, she and my teenaged self materialized before me.

"Don't you ever go home?" she asked. A wisp of her mahogany hair traced her flushed cheek and clung to her inviting lips. I remember feeling like a trespasser in a sacred place. The other me lifted his eyes and met hers. Calm, accepting, gentle, inclusive and blue, clear blue, I was mesmerized. In a moment, I'd planned a lifetime with her. "Where'd you go?"

Shaking my head, I responded. "What do you mean?"

"The look on your face... you looked like you were somewhere else," she answered.

"I was... umm... thinking about summer vacation," I lied, not wanting to admit that I was mentally building our first home together.

"Oh. Are you going somewhere special this year?" she asked.

Her gaze unraveling me from within, I strained to think of anything but those eyes. "Lake... blue... actually, I was thinking about last year's vacation. We hiked to Egypt Lake. I was actually thinking about the lake and how..." The inner battle commenced, part of me wanting to tell her how the majesty of the lake paled in comparison to her own deep reservoirs of loveliness, part of me far preferring the defensive position of not putting myself out there too far.

"How what?" she asked.

My internal war waged on, the combatants too evenly matched for anything but a compromise. "How pretty it was," I said, trying to say with my eyes what I was not saying with my mouth.

"Is there something wrong with your eye? It's twitching a little," she said.

"Umm, it's a disease... I mean diseased, but its not contagious so you don't have to leave," I said.

"Egypt Lake sounds very nice. Maybe I'll have to go see it some time," she said.

It was as good as if she had placed her hand out there, right in perfect position for me to grab it. I hoped this was an invitation, and yet the struggle within me remained unresolved. "You should it's great."

"Okay," she said, "I should probably get back to the game. My brother is going to be up to bat pretty soon."

I really wanted to tell her she could watch from here. I really wanted to tell her why I was thinking about that lake. But I also really didn't want to be rejected. If I could only come up with something that would let her know how I felt about her. "Okay. Come back soon. I'll give you a fifteen percent discount, no twenty."

"Bye, Taven," she said, then turned away and walked towards the game.

All I wanted to do was to call over to her. If she would turn around, just a little, it would be a sign she was interested. I knew I should have offered at least fifty percent. If it wasn't for operating costs, I'd have given them to her for free. Actually if I knew she was interested, operating costs or not, she would be getting them for free. I wondered if she would feel bribed if I offered her free hot dogs to go on a date with me.

"Was I really that lame?" I asked myself, still watching it all unfold. But I understood because I wasn't just watching, I was experiencing. I seemed to be linked emotionally to the me in the vision. I felt the awkwardness, the uncertainty and the tractor-beam like tug towards her. At that moment I wanted to be hers, and wanted for her to be mine, more than anything. But fear overcame what I really wanted. "Just tell her how you feel. How I feel."

"Taven." She hadn't turned around. Was she the one calling me? "Taven." Maybe it was her. Maybe this was my chance to change things, although I wasn't quite sure what I'd be changing... maybe to make it work between us. "Taven. Taven. Taven!"

Eve, the baseball team, the people in the stands, the field and my vending cart transitioned to a familiar face well within my personal bubble, although a name didn't immediately attach itself to the woman to whom the face belonged. She knelt next to me, her hands on my shoulders. I couldn't feel them but was unable to sit up because of the pressure they put on me.

"Did you rescue me from that guy?" I asked.

"I'm not sure what you're talking about. You were lying down having a mighty fine nap when I found you."

"Were you looking for me?"

"Don't you know who I am?" she asked.

I stared at her. In no way did she remind me of Eve, but since she was the only one I could think of, I asked tentatively, "Eve?"

"No dear, try again," she responded.

"Can you give me a hint?" I responded.

"I used to babysit you when you were a little boy," she responded.

Vague remembrances of babysitters from days gone by floated in my consciousness. I worried I was in purgatory because if the only person looking for me was one of my babysitters, who I regularly tortured, things were likely not going to go well for me. I wasn't bad. I was, as my mom put it, energetic. And so a water fight in the house, wrestling the babysitter on the front lawn, lighting things on fire in the backyard were average activities when the babysitter was over.

Before I could answer, she asked, "Do you remember Colonel?"

Colonel? Colonel. Colonel! I closed my eyes. The woman faded from view. I saw myself as a little boy toddling in the grass in front of a bungalow blanketed in sparkling white stucco, red shudders adorning its windows. A portly elderly woman opened the door, with a face a judge might not give first prize for beauty but which warmed my heart to see it, dressed neatly in a floral patterned dress that hung below her knees, her feet shod in fluffy slippers. Before she could restrain it, a black and white powder keg of a dog flew out of the door, charged me and knocked me to the ground, pinning me and bathing my face with its spit.

This memory faded from view and was replaced again by this familiar and pleasing face. "Auntie Sophie?"

"You remembered me. Oh, my little boy, how I've missed you," she said, still kneeling beside me as she pulled me by my shoulders into a seated position.

I knew it was Auntie Sophie despite the fact she had lost all her wrinkles and looked like she was in her twenties. The same way I used to know who Grandma and Grandpa were when I looked at old pictures of them. Certain things didn't change and I could recognize them in the person no matter how old the person got. I recognized her crooked smile and the tone of her voice, now stronger and clearer than it was then. It was also helpful that she was wearing the same type of floral patterned dress she used to wear.

It was at that moment that I realized again, that I was dead. Sophia Reeve, my great grandmother's sister, died when I was five years old. Her face was suddenly more serious. I said "I'm sorry about what I did to Colonel."

"Oh don't worry about it. I'm sure Old Colonel's gotten over the paint job you gave him."

The fleeting film-like image of that crazy dog tearing around the front lawn with a green lightning blotch on its side was almost enough to make me to laugh. I shook my head and the memory dropped from view and there I was again, sitting by my great great auntie who was doting over me as though I was a baby again.

The strange thing was that when I remembered something, it was like high definition, but being with the young-looking Auntie Sophie, wherever that was, was like regular cable. And it wasn't only her that was less watchable. The entire clearing in which we sat was off again, like it was when I first arrived in the field.

I wanted to ask her why she looked weird, but wisely realized, after attempting to compose the question in my mind, that asking a woman why she looked weird, no matter how you did it, was rude. I decided to ask something more fundamental, something for which I was pretty certain of the answer. "Am I dead? But before you answer, do you think… maybe… you could back up a little?"

"Oh sorry," she said, lowering the fingers with which I was sure she would pinch my cheek, "I was so excited to see my little Tay Tay again. Okay, now, your question, are you dead. My dear, the answer, well, it depends on what you mean by that."

"What do you mean by what do I mean by that? What else could dead mean?" I asked.

She smoothed out the corners of her dress. "Being dead means all sorts of different things. So what is it that makes you ask if you are dead?"

"I mean is me being dead the reason I can't feel anything… with my fingers or hands or face?" I asked.

"Yes it is. Your body is dead," she answered.

Having concluded on my own that I was dead, I was surprised how hearing her tell me was like being told I hadn't made the varsity basketball team despite the fact all of my friends had.

"Are you alright, Taven?" she asked.

She was already treating me like a baby. The last thing I wanted was a gush of emotions to prove it. "So what other kinds of dead are there?"

"There are some, in this world, that died before ever living, and some that died after dying. You can't help your body dying. That's the way it was built. But your hopes, your dreams, your love, you can keep from dying." Her gaze bore into me, like a sudden bright light into a dark room. "Are you alive?"

I closed my eyes and I was caught up in a swirling transformation of my hazy surroundings into a darkened room, occasionally pierced by multi-colored strobe lights, pounded by music, dripping with teenage angst: the school dance. I was hovering over the dance floor, seeing my living self against the wall, pitifully casting glances at Eve as she danced with a group of friends, dancing as though she and the music were one. Watching her was like hearing the music.

I was never much for dancing, well; truthfully, I was never much for the constant threat of rejection. When I did go, I usually found a particularly comfortable chair next to the wall and hoped someone would ask me to dance. That was another of my problems, the link between my feet and the beat had never been properly connected, so if I did dance, I usually went with the slight head bob for fast songs and the safety sway for the slow ones.

When the song ended and the girls shared a giggle and Eve made straight for me, it didn't matter that I couldn't dance. I saw myself grip the chair in amazement and felt the same anticipation all over again.

And then it was over. Like water sucked out of a toilet, I was flushed out the memory and Auntie Sophie was still looking at me, clearly waiting for the answer to her question. "I feel alive when I close my eyes."

"What is it that makes you feel alive?" As I focused back on her, thoughts of Auntie Sophie, one piece at a time, fit themselves together. I remembered that Mom and Dad told me that Auntie Sophie had never been married and had had no children. That didn't stop her from being my favorite aunt. I also remembered the same was true of all her nephews and nieces, her great nephews and nieces and her great great nephews and nieces. She was still on the floor playing with the toddlers into her extreme age. I was comfortable with her, but not enough to share my feelings for Eve so I shrugged an *I don't know* as my response.

"I know this is all very overwhelming, but you'll find the answer to the question absolutely liberating. Do you feel dead?"

I really wasn't sure what dead was supposed to feel like but if it was being invisible and ignored then I felt dead. But despite some very obvious differences, like not being able to feel anything, I really didn't feel any less conscious. If anything, as memories returned, I experienced awareness vividly. What's more I was talking, thinking, moving.

"I don't know. I guess I feel about sixty-three percent alive and thirty-seven percent dead."

She sniggered. "Oh, Taven, you were always such a funny boy. Even as a little guy. You were always up to something that was bound to cause a laugh or get you in trouble. Memory is a beautiful thing here. I like your outfit."

"Thanks. I was pleasantly surprised to have clothes rather than being issued a toga and a harp. You always have to worry about how you're sitting in that type of outfit. Like, do you cross your legs or just hold them close together?"

Her laugh rang out. "Knees together... Toga... harp..." Still chuckling, she stood and took several steps away from me, walking the same way I remembered. She had a bad knee toward the end of her life and she relied very heavily on a cane to walk. Each left step was a long pause and pivoting motion to the right leg.

"Does your knee still bother you?" I asked.

"Nope. One of the wonderful changes. No pain," she answered, as she leaned over and patted her knees.

"Then why are you walking like that?"

"Like what?"

"You know, with your limp." Immediately following my question, she walked in a small circle, paying special attention to the way she walked.

"I didn't even notice I was walking that way. Who knows how long I've been walking around like that when I didn't need to," she said as she straightened up and began walking normally. She turned to face me now about ten paces away from me. "Thank you for letting me know. It'd have been nice if your great auntie Janice would have told me I was still walking like that but she's always too worried about hurting someone's feelings. You'd think she'd be willing to help me out seeing that I changed her diaper when she was a baby."

"Great Auntie Janice?"

"Don't you remember her? She and Peter lived on a farm not far from you. We used to like to get together now and then and compare notes about our experience here before she moved on."

"The farm with all the chickens and the stinky cows?" I asked.

"I guess you can call the cows whatever you want, but, yes, they're the ones with the chickens and the cows," she responded, moving closer to me again.

"Where did great aunt Janice go? Did great uncle Peter go with her?" I asked.

"They are together. They moved on together," Auntie Sophie said.

"Moved on?" I asked.

"You'll figure it out soon enough, but we don't stay here forever. Some stay longer, some shorter. It's never all that clear as to why some stay longer than others, but the gist is that when it's your time, it's your time," she answered.

"Is moving on like dying is, I mean like when our body dies?"

"I guess in a way, but not really. When our physical bodies die, we are almost entirely cut off from the ones we leave behind. Although we don't get to see them all the time, family and friends that have moved on can come visit us now and then. From what I've been told by your great great great grandpa Regus it's like having a body, but not having to worry about it staying alive, getting hurt or getting sick. Being able to touch again, feel with fingers again, smell with my nose and not just comprehend the smell."

"How does great great grandpa..."

"There are three greats."

"Right. How does great great great grandpa Regus know?" I asked.

"He's moved on too," she said.

"And he visited you," I asked.

"He did shortly after I arrived here. He did the same type of thing that I'm doing for you. Helped me understand and get acclimatized to the concept of this change. And to give a warning," she said, her tone becoming more serious.

"What warning?" I asked.

"Don't stop growing," she said.

"Like taller?" I asked, trying to be funny.

"Funny boy," she tousled my hair, "It's easy to stop moving forward without a body. You've got to resist settling in."

I wasn't sure how to respond to that but the fuzziness of everything was very distracting. "I think my eyes are broken. I got them working before, but I'm not sure how I did it. Everything looks blurry."

"You're seeing what you didn't see before Taven. This world has layers. Not having a body helps a person to experience them. Look again, but focus beyond what you see, kind of cross your eyes, except try not to see with your eyes," she said.

"How are you supposed to do that?"

"You'll know it when you do. You will be looking, you will be focusing, but it's your mind that will take you where you need to go."

I had no idea how to look without using my eyes. Not knowing what else to do, but knowing there was something I wasn't seeing, I focused on the idea there was something I was not seeing in this park. As it had before, everything was back in high definition, and materializing around me were dozens of people walking, running and playing. On the other side of the path was a kid's paradise, a sturdy wooden park, slide, monkey bars, swings, and swinging bridges. After two big pushes, hands on his back, a woman ran behind and eventually under a young boy on the swings. Gloria was there again. She climbed the stairs to the slide and squealed as she went down. Not seeming to be having near the same degree of fun, determined runners slogged past each other up and down the path.

A boy and a man walked slowly up the path, fishing rods in hand. I remembered the time my dad took me fishing at Red Lodge Park. The memory was sweet. To savor it, I closed my eyes. And I was there, watching myself and my dad. He gave me half of a large pop bottle and sent me to the shallows where he showed me the schools of minnows swimming, their shadows trailing them on the water's bed. Hunched over on the border of the stream, I scooped them up and put them back. The memory swept through experience without regard to time and I knew the memory was drawing to a close. The younger version of me asked Dad if I could take some home with me. He told me if I did, they'd all die a lot sooner then if I let them be alive here. I had decided to bring them anyway, but the look my mom gave me made it clear I was not, regardless of what I chose, bringing the fish home in the van. Dumping the fish and the water back into the stream, the younger version of me stomped to the van.

More than anything, at that moment, I wanted climb into that van, and go home with my family.

"Taven?" a voice called, as I watched the van drive away.

"Yes, Mom?"

"No, it's not your mother. Come back," Auntie Sophie's voice called.

It was like waking up too early from a nap. Before I knew it I was back in the heavily populated clearing. "I don't want to. It's so nice here. It feels like it used to."

"Come back," she said again. No one seemed to be bothered by the bodiless voice, other than me.

"But I was with my family."

"As nice as old memories are, remembering is fine only so long as you are making new memories. The park's too busy in the mortal world so come on back. Besides, I'd appreciate it if you weren't somewhere else at the same time I was talking to you."

"How do I get back?"

"Focus on the sound of my voice and look at it."

I wasn't too sure how you went about looking at a sound, but it was surprisingly easy to do. No sooner had I directed my attention to Auntie Sophie's voice, I was seated on the ground alone with my auntie in the quiet clearing, back in blurred cablevision.

I stood up which took no effort at all. I had to decide to stand, and move my legs, but there was no muscular strain, no difficulty at all in standing on my feet. "I have a few questions."

"I'm sure you do, but before you ask them and now that you're on your feet, come give your auntie a hug."

I walked towards her and embraced her. I didn't feel the texture of the floral patterned dress, nor the press of her body aside from the fact that I couldn't be pulled any closer into her. But I felt warmth, not a physical sensation, but a glow within me. I closed my eyes and I was a little boy, tightly embraced in her arms, the smell of her perfume surrounding me. I opened my eyes, surprised at the vividness of the experience, and disappointed that my new world was not nearly so pleasing to the senses.

"I love you," she said.

"Love you too," I said, hesitating at the commitment but despite my hesitation, I was surprised at how it immediately intensified the bond I felt with her.

"As much as I'd like to keep you all to myself, I guess I should probably let everyone know I've found you," she said.

"Everyone?" I asked, excited at the prospects of who I would now meet.

With her eyes closed, she whispered, "Taven's here."

The impromptu family reunion

No sound to mark their arrival, familiar people appeared out of nowhere. My brain stopped short of identifying them beyond being members of the White family.

In no time, these unknown familiars surrounded me, smiling and waving, keeping their distance but too close for comfort. I stood there, the bulls-eye in the middle of a target, everyone staring. In unison, the group broke their gaze, turned to the right or the left and started talking to the person next to them. If it wasn't for the fact that I was trapped in the middle, I'd have made a run for the river.

A large bearded man dressed like a lumberjack, walked straight toward me, arms spread wide. "Taven!"

"Hi." I could not place his face. "I'm really sorry. You look so familiar but I can't remember who you are."

"No need to be ashamed of anything," he boomed lowering his arms as he stopped short of me. "Transitioning is not an easy process. But you'll figure it out, you're a White."

I'd heard him say that to me before. "Uncle Bennett?"

"Alive and kicking."

But that's not the way I remembered him. I was only ten when he died. Ten was an exceptionally hard year for me. The friends I had made were being shuffled into different cliques, as though chance was deciding what their soon to be teenage experience would be like. I, on the other hand, resisted the shuffling. I didn't like to be labeled but not being labeled left me alone.

Uncle Bennett was literally half of what he was as he laid on the hospital bed. After I had expressed my concerns on a visit to him in the hospital, he listened to me then whispered the same words to me as I stared at the floor. "But you'll figure it out, you're a White." I was quickly out of the memory and back to the man, no longer bound to the hospital bed and clearly alive and kicking.

I met my uncle halfway and hugged him.

"Not quite what you expected is it?" he asked.

I couldn't remember enough to know what it was that I expected. If nothing else, being here was nothing but unexpected. "I guess so."

"Isn't it amazing how much you can get done when you don't have to worry about being alive? With all my spare time I've been enjoying regular visits to ancient Mesopotamia."

I didn't know whether I should ask what, when or where. All that came out was, "That's great."

"You haven't visited another time or place yet, have you? I think I had travel figured out within minutes of getting here," he said with a wink.

"I guess I traveled to a place with tall buildings and strange people."

"You mean your walk downtown? I don't want to hurt your feelings, my boy, but I wouldn't call that traveling."

He laughed but I only smirked. I wasn't ready to find humor in the experience. Not yet any way. I wanted to ask him what he meant by traveling but I already felt dumb for not figuring it out on my own. Asking him was only going to make it worse. "So where were you again?"

"Mesopotamia. I had to see first-hand goat pee used as facial hair gel before trying it in my own beard. You know, to stiffen the curls. Do you think I'd look good with a rock-hard curly beard?" he asked.

The laugh forced its way out, and I felt relieved when it did. "Umm, no," I responded. "But I'm not really a beard kind of guy."

"You really ought to try it sometime. It's a real sign of manhood. You have hit puberty, haven't you? It's hard to tell with that baby face of yours," he said, giving my cheek a pat.

"I'm dead. Can I even grow a beard anymore?"

"That's a defeated way to look at the situation. If you've learned anything by being here, it has to be that you're not dead. Just no longer in the same sphere of existence. But if I couldn't grow a beard, maybe I'd want to be..."

"Don't you mind him, Taven. He's just trying to get a rise out of you," Auntie Sophie consoled, as she shuffled me towards the border of the circle. "That is a man that was very happy to find out that death wasn't the end of him. The thought of the conclusion of existence nagged him all those days in the hospital. And then in the blink of an eye, those worries were no more than a failed hypothesis."

"I thought he was pretty funny."

"You don't know the half of it. He spends most his time watching a young sheepherder from another time and place. If that's not funny, I don't know what is."

"Have you asked him why?"

"Why what?" asked Uncle Bennett. I turned to look and saw his massive hand on my shoulder.

"He's feeling overwhelmed. He's trying to figure things out," Auntie Sophie responded, unable to tear me from Uncle Bennett's grip. "Try to be as helpful as you can be."

I turned to Uncle Bennett. "What's the real reason you go to Mesopawhosawhatsit?"

Uncle Bennett did not blink. "There's a shepherd boy I'm studying."

"Why?"

Uncle Bennett clapped his hands. "Do you know how long I've been waiting for someone to ask me? Instead I get the weird looks and the quiet whispers. Conversations that stop the minute the participants think I'm close enough to hear. This beard is a sound amplifier. It's not actually but it is very manly. Don't you think?"

"Oh, very manly," said Auntie Sophie.

"Yes, manly." I offered. "But you didn't answer my question."

"Patience my boy. Anything worth knowing requires patience to obtain it."

"Okay."

Uncle Bennett stared at me. I wondered whether he had a number he was counting down to, that would be an indicator that I'd been patient enough. "Are you ready now?"

Auntie Sophie sighed. "Yep." I answered.

"I've been watching a young boy tending his ailing father's goats on a quiet hill not far from his father's tent. He's never learned to read, and frankly, has no concept of why you would need to. Every morning he walks out, leading his herd to pasture, sitting quietly, sometimes singing a song his father probably taught him, who had probably learned it from his father and so on." I waited for the punch line, but I could see from the far off look in his eyes that this was not part of a joke. "He knows the habits of each of his goats and treats them as close friends, often quietly speaking with them. He's ten years-old, but so responsible."

"How do you…" I began until jerked with surprising force to face the vaguely familiar face of Great Aunt Mercy. I was really glad I couldn't feel the wet slobbery kiss she planted on me, although it stimulated the memory of them from my childhood enough to make me shiver.

"Are you cold, dear?" she asked.

"No… umm… I mean I'm just getting used to being dead… I mean not alive… you know, I don't know what I mean."

She patted my cheek. Her face was so much younger than I remembered it. If it wasn't for her eyes I wouldn't have recognized her. "You always were such a spunky, guy." She leaned in to my ear. "Don't tell your cousins but you were always my favorite."

"Thanks, Auntie Mercy." She was closely followed by great grandpa John Johnson, a tall, stern-looking man with a goatee, who was accompanied by great grandma Marie Toone.

"And how are you Johnny?" asked great grandpa John Johnson. The trio completely hedged me off from Uncle Bennett and Auntie Sophie. I was happy enough to see everyone else, but I felt like someone had taken my safety blanket from me, not that I was still dependent on it. At least I didn't think I was.

I had never met great grandpa John Johnson, but knew the story well. When I was born there was an expectation on both sides of the family that my name would be John. That was dad's name, and coincidentally the first name of both of my grandfathers, and two of my great grandfathers. I was told there was a mix of relief and disappointment, ranging from, *at least no one will be able to make toilet jokes about him like we can about the rest of you guys* to great grandpa John Johnson who was quite sure my parents had made an irreversibly critical error in naming me, saying, "Sounds more like a bird than a man."

"It's Taven, great grandpa," I said, "and I guess I'm doing pretty good, considering the circumstances."

"I still like John better. He looks like a John to me, don't you think Marie?"

"I'm not sure he'd live up to the name," interrupted great great grandpa John White. Somehow I knew who he was the instant I saw him. Unlike everyone else who seemed to have regained youth, he looked like he was ninety-two. He wore broad suspenders to keep his pants at the bottom of his ribcage. "Spending time downtown. That's says a lot in itself. And how long was he sitting in that river for?"

"I wasn't issued an instruction book when I got here," I mumbled. I was so focused on this great grandpa that I didn't realize the others slink away. In fact I wouldn't have noticed at all if it weren't for Marie Toone's thumbs up as she backed up.

"Look. We realize that this is all very overwhelming for you. Believe it or not, we've all been where you are and we know what you are feeling. Unlike you, most of the rest of us were interested in someone other than ourselves."

"I don't know what you mean?"

"Of course you don't. Why didn't you call for family? We would have come for you. Didn't you think we might want to see you?"

"I'm really not sure what I did wrong."

"If you don't like it... tough. There's one way to get what you want, and that is to learn it and to earn it," great great grandpa John White concluded with the family catch phrase.

"What are you talking about?"

"I know your type. You'll wander around and moan about until someone tells you exactly what you have to do to make it in this world. Pathetic. No initiative."

I was at a loss for words. Partly because I was shocked and partly because I had no idea why he was tearing into me.

"Nothing to say? Just what I thought. Lazy and no backbone." He turned and walked away from me. Auntie Sophie approached me and said, "Taven, don't worry too much about great great grandpa. He was a hard man in life. Changing is no easy task. Water flows easily down old ruts. But there's no denying he's a great leader."

"A great leader? If he's the leader, I don't want any part of this group," I said.

Moving on

"Can I have your attention please?" asked great great grandpa John White, mere moments since our encounter. I had hoped when Auntie Sophie moved me away from him, it was the last I'd hear from him for a while. It was clear from the immediate attention he received that he was regarded, by this crowd at least, with respect. "Taven is not the only reason we are here today," he paused allowing the anticipation to take its full effect. "I have received notice that one among us will be moving on. We are also here to see our Sophie off."

"Is she going on vacation?" I asked, hoping to make life a little more difficult for good old great great grandpa, however, all I did was provoke several of my dead relatives to shake their heads, while others held their fingers over their lips to shush me like I was two years-old.

He, however, acted as though I had not spoken, or possibly not existed, and continued, "I am grateful for our dear Sophie. Many..." he paused and with a pained look in his eyes continued, "including me, judged her in life. We judged her for failing to get married. We judged her for her long unmarried years. We judged her because she was just fine with the way things had worked out for her. But now look at her. She was and is a great protector of our children, living and dead. She has sought them out in their time of need. Just as she has now done with Taven, she has assisted those wayfaring and confused among us to find the way."

Apparently I not only had the wrong name but also was wayfaring and confused. Maybe great great grandpa thought I was confused because I didn't wear my pants up to my armpits like he did.

"I will always be grateful for the work she has done among us. Her appointment to move on is well earned and I feel honored to be the deliverer of the message," he continued.

"Oh, John," Auntie Sophie stammered, "You're exaggerating. What good have I ever done?"

No sooner had Auntie Sophie objected than a light began to shine through her. She wasn't translucent but she emanated light. "I never thought it would happen to me. I never thought it would happen to me. How wonderful," Auntie Sophie exclaimed. She turned towards me, winked a twinkling eye, and said, "I can feel my fingers," and was gone.

My mouth hung open, all the questions I wanted to ask crowded at the back of my throat, the possibility of asking them shrinking with the disappearance of my relatives one by one. When great great grandpa White hobbled over I thought I would receive a little explanation despite his gruffness before. "Great great grandpa White?"

He held his hand up to stop me, and said, "Call me Chief and," he looked me from head to toe, "don't be a waste of space." He was gone before I could offer the same suggestion back to him.

I was alone with Uncle Bennett. "She's moved on," he said. "Auntie Sophie. That's why she left."

That was not the foremost question on my mind. "Why didn't you stand up for me?"

"Pardon me?"

"When Chief was tearing into me, you stood there and let him do it. What gives him the right to say what he said to me and how could he tear into me and then announce Auntie Sophie moving out?"

"It's moving on. That's a lot of questions. Which ones do you want the answer for and which ones were for venting purposes only?" he responded.

"All of them."

"All of them were venting?"

"No. I would like answers for all of them."

"Let me start out with a question for you. Why didn't you stand up for yourself?" he asked.

"Because he's my great great grandpa," I answered.

"That's my reason too. Doesn't make it right, but don't read too much into it. Don't throw away everything that was said without trying to figure out if there's some truth to it."

"Are you saying I'm lazy? A waste of space?"

"No. I didn't say what he said was accurate as it was said, but maybe you can find some truth in it, if not about yourself, then maybe about him. For the record, I think you're great." He tucked me under his arm and squeezed.

"Thanks. What happened to Auntie Sophie?"

"Nothing happened to her and you should know it wasn't John White that changed her. He was the messenger only, a privilege he holds because someone else gave it to him. Auntie Sophie became. She moved on."

"I don't understand. What does moving on mean?"

"Ah, good question, but that's one for you to figure out. No good ruining a good surprise. And even if I was inclined to ruin your surprise, I couldn't because I don't know. Only way you find out is by being the one to lead." Uncle Bennett released me from his grip and took two steps away from me. "I've really got to go. If you've got questions, I'd make them good."

"What do you mean you've got to go? What am I supposed to do?"

"Remember to look for that grain of truth. And, stay out of dreams. Good luck." Without even a wave of his hand he was gone and I was alone in my hazy reality.

I focused on the mortal world, hoping that's where everyone had disappeared to, that this was some type of test. Traveling from the alternate world to the mortal world was becoming second nature and I was there the instant I determined to be there. My satisfaction was short-lived. The clarity of the moonlit park only emphasized the fact that the song of the crickets was my only companion.

"I'm here. Don't leave me alone. What am I supposed to do?" I yelled. "Why are you doing this to me? Why are you leaving me alone? Is anybody there?"

Silence.

I travelled back to the alternate world and back to the mortal one. I closed my eyes hoping to discover some way of finding my family, some way of connecting with them. Instead of the back of my eyelids, it seemed as though I stood at the edge of a cliff overlooking an endless body of water. Thousands of living scenes danced on its surface. Although they were far below me, I saw each of them clearly. In many of the images I recognized myself at varying ages all the way up to the end of my teen-age years. I was at birthday parties with my family, learning to ride a two-wheel bike, my first and last days of elementary, junior high and senior high school and driving around with my best friend Carl.

No sooner had I spotted Carl than I felt an overwhelming desire to leap off of the cliff and back into my life. All reason had fled, only fear kept my toes at the threshold of oblivion. It was too far to fall. I'd die. But I couldn't die; I was already dead, wasn't I? I leapt.

Gone were the cliff and the lake. I hovered over my sixteen year-old self, able to see everything that was going on as though the top of the car was translucent.

Driving was my best friend Carl. We were on the way home from basketball practice.

"You're going to look like you're stalking her," the sixteen year-old me said.

"Look. I'm just trying to help you out. If you'd just ask her out, I wouldn't have to keep driving you past her house," said Carl.

"I'm all sweaty from practice. I smell bad. I'll call her later," I responded.

"How's that different from any other time? Call her," he insisted, "or I'll drive you right up to her house and won't move until you get out and ask her out."

"I can't just call her. I've got to figure out what we're going to do first."

"You'll have two minutes to figure it out because we're going to her house right now," he said, as he pulled a U-turn.

"Turn the car around. Take me home," I reached for the steering wheel.

"You're just chicken," he said, brushing my hand away from the steering wheel.

"I'm not chicken... I smell bad," I said, reaching for the wheel again.

"All you have to do is go up to the door. Say something cool, like, I was so excited to ask you out that I came stinky."

"Right. I'm sure she'd be really impressed by the fact I have no regard for personal hygiene." I said. "We'll see her in school tomorrow. I'll ask her then."

Carl rolled his eyes. "Yah right. I'm just trying to help you out and I'm tired of hearing you whine about her."

"I don't whine about her," I said.

"Maybe you should stop being lame and go ask her out, come on. Her street's right here. I can't help myself. I'm turning in," he said as he put both hands on the wheel, directing the car right at her house.

His guard hand now being on the steering wheel, sixteen year-old me grabbed the one o'clock position of the wheel and pushed it away from me. We jolted back onto the street, and careened past the yellow line and into oncoming traffic; Carl forced the wheel in the other direction, failing to take into account the fact we had now passed the cul-de-sac. The passenger side wheels of the car went over the sidewalk and onto a bit of the public green space. We did stop short of the tree though. And that's when we heard the siren and saw the red and blue lights.

"What should I do?" Carl half yelled, half cried.

"Get off the curb and..." I stopped when I saw Eve was walking towards us. She was with a few of her friends. We couldn't hide. I slumped into my seat. Carl popped the gearshift into reverse and started to back up. If she hadn't seen us yet, the honk of the police officer's car drew her attention to us.

Undeterred by the police car or our position in front of the tree, she approached the car. "Carl, is everything okay? Taven?"

"Hi," I blurted.

"We're fine," Carl groaned.

"How did you guys end up on the curb? Were you in an accident or something?" Carl opened his mouth but closed it when I elbowed him in the side. "Okay. Well I hope you guys aren't in too much trouble. I'd better get going, the policeman is headed over."

"Do you want to go out with me?" I stammered.

"I've got a bunch of friends coming to my house..."

I interrupted her. "Never mind. I'm very busy. We'll probably be headed to jail after this."

Carl pushed me. "The policeman is almost to our window. Why on earth would you say we're going to go to jail? You grabbing my wheel so we could avoid her house is why we're going to get in trouble. We didn't do anything else."

"But..." I turned back to Eve who was no longer at my window and, in the midst of a huddle of girls, was now walking by the police car. "I told you I would ask her."

"You were all over the road back there," the police officer said in a cold, justice-like voice.

"I'm sorry officer," said Carl.

"Have you been drinking?" he asked, more frostily, if that was even possible, than his first question.

"No, sir. Taven grabbed the wheel and I over corrected," Carl said pointing at me.

"Is that true?" the policeman asked.

"I just didn't want to go where he was driving," I answered.

"That's no excuse. You could have seriously injured yourselves or that group of girls that walked by…"

What does this have to do with anything? No sooner had the thought occurred but I was detached from the embarrassing police interrogation. The sixteen year-old me and Carl sat there, not nearly so lucky. The scene played before me but the sound was muted and I could again differentiate between myself and the me in the memory.

The familiar yearning for Eve remained in my heart. I wondered how all I wanted at that moment was her, when there was now no way of being with her. She was alive and I was dead. Hopelessness gripped me. I didn't want to feel anymore. I was being tortured by what would have been my great satisfaction, if she would ever have been mine.

It was as though a forked path loomed before me, one path predictable, well worn, and the other unknown - it was for me to choose and decide what I would be. I did not hesitate long because my dominating thought was that I could not honor what could have been by becoming what never could have possessed it. I had a path to walk. My existence, I decided then and there, was not going to rot in sweet and bitter nostalgia. And that's when I figured out how I was going to find out where everyone went, where Bennett went, where Sophie went.

All I had to do was relive my memory of meeting my relatives. I could watch it as many times as it took to figure out what was going on and to get the information I needed. I took one last look at the shame-faced sixteen year old me and then to the sky. To my relief, I was immediately drawn to the cliff's edge and to the moonlit images across the water's surface. I looked in vain for anything that was associated with my experience in death. No flowing banners. No day in the river. No awkward and confusing family reunion. No female rescuer. No Bennett and no Sophie.

In the world within my mind, I soon found no exploration beyond what I could see on the surface of the water was possible. My feet were rooted in the ground. My attempts to glance about me only found me gazing once again at the water's surface.

Although I did not see the immediate solution to the problem, I knew there were avenues for travel and all I had to do was find them. I opened my eyes.

Alone in my hazy field, I did not feel lost but I knew I needed to find someone to show me the way. And I was pretty sure I knew where I could find someone.

Something seems familiar

"You!" Elmer cried. "Get him!"

"Look. I'm sorry about what I said before. I really need your help," I said as a dozen or so bodies surrounded me, making it impossible to move or see beyond them, until two stepped away, giving way to Elmer. Standing on the cliff, searching out the one person I was pretty sure would be findable seemed like a really good idea. Now it didn't seem like a good idea at all. He struck me in the stomach.

"I don't know who you think you are to get someone like that woman involved in our business. You made this all very personal," he said, stepping back.

"What? I don't know what you're talking about."

"Don't play dumb with me," he said. Usually this would be an invitation to explain the misunderstanding, but it wasn't. Before I could inhale, he struck me across the face. My cheek felt as though it was blistered and charred and he was winding up to hit me again. I wasn't sure what his long term goals were but I was not going to hang around to find out. I focused on the blurry otherworld.

The visored-man and his goons and the contents of the mall were gone. Still huddled over, I waited for the him to follow me here and pummel me. But he didn't come.

The building that housed the mall, once imposing and central to the landscape, was now shady and translucent, visible but not tangible. Everything that would have been on the outside, on a busy down town day was gone. No trucks, no people, no vendors, nothing that I could see.

I stepped up to the shadow of the exterior wall of the building nearest me and reached out, and like smoke, its border fled at the touch of my hand. It was like standing in the middle of a gigantic tent made of smoke. Grass covered the ground. Within a few moments, the shadowy exterior of the buildings had evaporated into nothing. I was alone.

"Auntie Sophie?" I shouted against hope. "Uncle Bennett?"

I walked toward the hazy trees in the distance but when it seemed that they withdrew from me as I approached them, I stopped. I knew I needed help and I had no idea how to contact family. All that was left was to go back to where I knew there were others like me. Back downtown. I'd avoid Elmer and approach someone else. If I was patient enough I'd find someone. I focused and found that I was no longer on one of the busy down town streets.

I was now on a narrow two-lane road with no line down the middle, the road dividing rows of houses on either side. It was nighttime, the light of the street lamps making it impossible to see any but the brightest of the stars. None of the houses were all that large, nor were they adorned with anything but durable rather than opulent adornments. The yards were well kept and the gardens well tended. The place radiated familiarity. It felt like home.

Stepping off the road onto the sidewalk, I walked, hoping that fate had brought me where I longed to be. I hoped against hope that somehow I was where Mom and Dad were.

Walking in the stillness of the night, I came upon a house, with a large poplar tree in the front, a paved parking pad on the edge of the lawn, a waist high hedge dividing the property from the neighbors. Tan brown, white door, brown trimming, this was home, it had to be. It was so familiar; however, the actual memory of the place escaped me.

I approached the front door and attempted to open it, forgetting I could not open a door in the mortal world. Even if I could, the door would probably be locked, as it was the middle of the night. "Open the door, it's me, Taven!" I shouted. I attempted to push the doorbell but nothing happened.

Circling the house, eyes scanning for any form of entry point, I unnecessarily crept in the shadows. The small rectangular vent jutting out of the side of the house, a little larger than my fist was the only opening. Given that I was less tangible in this new body, I thought I might be able to shimmy up but soon found I was unable to apply enough force to get myself up and in. I needed another way.

Hoping my inability to pass through walls had everything to do with a lack of faith, I ran at the house only to find that I was most unable to pass through a solid wall. Another failed attempt and another lesson learned.

I was now feeling desperate. I needed to get in. I needed to talk to my parents. They could help me. I wouldn't be alone. I unfocused and was back in the hazy world, the smoky frame of the house disappearing fast. I took one step beyond where I thought the wall would be and refocused.

Rather than standing in front of the familiar house, I was now on a completely different street, lined with townhouses with a shared front lawn, the grass long in places and sparse in others, thistles and dandelions the prominent vegetation.

I quickly unfocused then took one step backwards, hoping this would put me back in front of my house. Perhaps I'd still be locked out but I would simply wait until the morning. Once someone opened the door, I'd go in.

I refocused and found myself in the middle of a much broader road, which intersected with another broad road not far from where I stood. A large flat building was on my left. Supposing I had stepped too far back ward, I went back and forth, back and forth, finding myself in different places each time, never sure where I was. As the sun began to rise in the mortal world, I found myself on yet another unfamiliar street, surrounded by unfamiliar houses. At that point, I decided I would simply walk. If I walked long enough, I was sure to see the same familiar street with the familiar houses and the well-tended lawns.

I don't know how long I walked, but I didn't recognize a single place. It wasn't long before the only remaining option seemed to be to sit down and rest my forehead on my knees. And that's what I did.

"Are you lost?" It was woman's voice. I didn't budge. I figured if I raised my head I'd see some lady talking to a little wandering puppy. I wasn't going to get excited over a possibility only to be disappointed again. Why even try?

Next thing I knew, my head was being titled back and my breath was stolen by what I saw. Looking intently at me, with striking emerald eyes and long blond hair, so soft I was tempted to touch it, was a casually dressed young woman. "Are you lost?"

My tongue seemed attached to the roof of my mouth. By the time I was able to loose it, "You're pretty", rolled out.

"Of all the pick-up lines I've heard, that is a first." She stood up and extended a hand to me. "Labels don't matter much here, but it helps to have one, so you can call me Fiona."

"Mine's Taven. And no, it's not a girl's name. My parents are not hippies and I didn't change it from something boring like Stanley..." Fiona's lip curled. She did not look pleased to me. "Not that Stanley's a bad name... You don't know any one named Stanley do you?"

Both corners of her mouth were now turned down and her eyes were strangely bulging. Mind spinning more slowly than my lips were moving, I continued, "I knew a guy named Stanley he was the smartest guy in our class, but there was that one time he came to school sick and threw up all over the place. Then he still refused to go home, and ended up throwing up in the hallway. It looked like cottage cheese. So gross."

Fiona honked. At first I wasn't sure what that meant, in fact I flinched at the sound. But her once clamped mouth was now open, her eyes came alive as she honked more than once.

"Is that your laugh or are you hurt or something?" I asked with all the tact I could muster.

"It's been a real long time since I've laughed, Taven. I really appreciate it," she said, pulling me to my feet. In an instant the smile was gone, the appeal remained but an invisible gulf separated us. "You didn't answer my first question. Are you lost?"

"Umm... yes. Definitely. In more ways than one. The impromptu family reunion I was forced to attend left me more confused than before. My auntie moved out, my uncle went back to Mesopotusiwhatsit and my great great great great... I can't remember if it's three or four greats... thinks I'm scum. So am I lost? Yes. Am I confused? Most certainly. Was I crying when you came? The answer to that depends on whether you think that's a good thing or not."

"You were crying?" she asked.

"No. Just resting. I have no idea how things work here and can't even remember how I died. Those gaps in knowledge made me want to sit with my head on my knees and look like I was crying. Just look though." I paused. She looked at me as though I had a third ear growing on my forehead. But she was not leaving, so I asked, "This is going to sound kind of kindergarten-ish, but can you help me find my house?"

"How old are you? Seven?" Her laugh was icy this time and I hadn't worn a winter jacket, mitts or a hat. "You need help. My friends and I are more than willing to help a guy like you out."

I wondered if *a guy like me* was a good thing to her. She was very strange, but so were all the other dead people I'd met. At least she wasn't beating me or disappearing without giving me any help at all. "That's nice of you. Do you guys belong to a club or something?"

"The big guy over there by the house is Ben and the guy on the other side of the street is Dan."

Ben was a big guy, looked more like a brown bear than a man, except that his face, other than his chin and cheeks, was not covered in fur. He was dressed in coveralls. Dan on the other hand, reminded me more of a praying mantis, with his beady eye and long thin limbs, dressed in a silk dinner jacket and pants.

"Hi, fellas. Good to meet you. Ben, I like your facial hair, very comprehensive. Dan, slick jacket. Very... umm... slick."

They waved, but said nothing.

Eyeing me like I was hiding something, Fiona asked, "So why do you need our help to find your house?"

At that moment the only thing I wanted to hide was the fact that not only did I know how to get back to the house I thought was my house but that I didn't even remember if it actually was my house. "Every time I go into cable vision I end up no where near to where I left living land."

"What are you talking about?" she asked. Ben blinked slowly and Dan looked into the air.

"What I mean is, you know how when you cross your eyes you can go to the mortal world. Well, after meeting some of my extended relatives, they left without telling me where they went or how to really do anything. So, I figured if I couldn't ask them for help, I'd ask someone I knew. In my infinite wisdom, I went and found the guy who had beaten me up before, until I was saved by an unknown woman. It shouldn't have been a surprise that he still wanted to beat me up rather than help me so I focused on the place where everything's blurry.

"Once I did that everything disappeared I decided to go back. Downtown was the only place I knew there were people I could talk to but when I went back, I was on a street with a house that felt like it was mine. I didn't recognize it but it was so familiar. It was night so…"

Fiona held put her hand on my shoulder. "That was me."

"Pardon me?"

"I stopped that low life from hurting you. I don't know how anyone could hurt a person like you." As she said it there was only what I could describe as emptiness in her eyes. She shook her head slightly and focused on me. "I hate to break it to you, but your family left you high and dry."

"What do you mean?" I asked.

"I can't imagine anyone leaving a person alone to figure this world out without some help. It's like leaving a newborn baby to fend for itself. Things are different here, Taven. It's cruel that they would do this to you. Family doesn't work. It crumbles in life and corrupts in death."

"That's gloomy," I said.

Her eyes blazed with intensity as she spoke, "Think about what happened to you. Think about what your so-called great grandpa said to you. What kind of person does that? How is that supposed to help someone who needs all the support he can get? Even the woman who first met you. As soon as something better comes up for her she ditches you and leaves you with your crazy uncle."

"How do you know all that? I mean did you see everything. Did you see what happened with the dog..."

"You mean when it took a leak on your face?" grumbled Ben.

Fiona looked to Ben. In response, Ben looked at the ground. "I am here to help you. Ben, although stupid, is here to help you, as is Dan. We've been watching you for a while, we brought you back to the field after you were knocked unconscious. We were about to introduce ourselves when your relatives came. I hoped they would help you, but I knew better. It's worse here. People are only out for themselves. Being family provides a cloak for selfish intention."

It amazed me that someone who looked like her could be so cold, frosty cold. "Why are you so down on my family?"

"Why aren't you?" she returned.

"What do you mean?"

"Since you've been here, who's really taken the time to help you out?" she asked. Before I could answer, she did for me, "I did. We did. I'm tired of people losing their way because they are blind to the fact that people, alive or dead, are selfish. I'm helping you because I expect it will pay dividends for me. I think you're handsome and I hope you'll start having similar feelings for me. And I don't want to hear anything about love because all it is, is two people getting what they want. So we might as well be honest about it and honest about the fact that your family left you high and dry. And about the fact that you think I'm pretty."

I was stuck somewhere between offended and flattered. She was gorgeous. I couldn't remember ever having someone who looked like her show any kind of interest in me. The closest I got to Eve was the run-in with the traffic police. But I wasn't going down without a fight. "So what's in it for them?"

"Ben and Dan. The other thing you have to learn is that motivations in this world are very different from anything you may partially remember. Food doesn't matter, as I'm sure you've realized. Family doesn't matter, as I've explained to you. Relationships only matter as far as they really benefit all people involved. Knowledge is everything. If you know something other people want, they'll do just about anything for you."

My mind turned to Elmer. He definitely had no socially redeeming qualities but he sure had a healthy following of goons wanting to know how to do what he could do. "So what is it you know that they are so desperate for?"

"Who said its what I know," she said, "Besides, are you interested in what I know, or in me? I'd be disappointed, very disappointed, if you were only looking for a few facts."

I didn't feel the finger she placed on my chest, but tingles would be an understatement to describe what her touch was: thrilling, strangely desirable and at the same time uncomfortable.

"To show I'm a nice girl, I'll help you find your family. I wish I could convince you otherwise, but I guess you'll just have to find out the hard way. But no matter what happens, I want you to know I'm on your side. No strings attached." She circled around me. "Tell you what, let's start with the basics. Do you remember what the house looked like?"

"I think so," I said. No sooner had the words escaped my lips than the vague image of the house slowly appeared in my mind as though layers of dust were being blown away in the wind.

"Draw that picture in your mind, then concentrate on it."

The house was in my mind was now nearly visible. "Ok, I've got it."

"Did you draw it?"

"Umm, the house appeared in my mind. Is that what you mean?"

"No, that's not good enough. You've got to create it yourself, otherwise you aren't going anywhere."

"I know this is going to sound dumb, but how am I supposed to draw in my mind? Is there some kind of mental pen I should know about?" I asked sincerely, although I wouldn't be surprised if it sounded like I was joking.

"Come on, dude. Are you that helpless?" a deeper voice grumbled.

I opened my eyes. Fiona was standing behind me. I knew she was touching me because I felt the same electricity at the point of contact. As I turned my head, I caught a glimpse of her fiery glance towards Ben, who was now standing directly behind her with his hand on her. Maybe I was silly for thinking I had a shot with her. I looked over my other shoulder and saw Dan was right there too.

As though she had read my mind, Fiona spoke, "Taven, don't worry about these two. The only way we can go with you is if we are in contact with you. That's the only reason I'm letting these two anywhere near us. I'll need them and if they aren't in contact, finding us will not be easy for them. Don't worry about them, they're not as bad as they seem. Close your eyes. Draw the house in your mind. It's the only way we'll find your family."

"Okay." No sooner had I closed my eyes than a box of well used crayons, the primary colors were nearly worn down to the paper and some of the other colors were missing or broken, appeared.

"You've got to use your mind, Taven," came Fiona's voice. "Flailing around with your hands won't do any good."

"I'm doing my best. I…"

"Don't worry. The first time is always the hardest. Once you get it, it'll be like riding a bike, only much better," she explained. "You need to use your mind as though it is your hand."

"Okay." Unsure of the mechanics of using my mind as a hand, I limited the command to pick up the crayon to my mind, and to my surprise, the worn blue crayon hovered over the image of the house, that was also in my mind. Slowly tracing the outline of the poplar tree in the front yard, the long line of the hedges dividing the two yards, the strands of grass in the well-tended yard and the modest house, what looked like it should have come from a three year-old took shape.

Everything faded to black. I opened my eyes to see Fiona now crouching in front of me, still clinging to my shoulders, her face lit despite the midnight sky. "Well done."

"Umm, thanks," I said. She definitely did not see the picture in my head because if she did, she would not have congratulated me.

"Taven, do you know where you are?" she asked me, smiling.

The light from the lamppost was sufficient to allow me to see the familiar well-tended row of houses clearly. I was standing in front of what I was sure was my parent's home. "We're here. How did you know how to do that?"

Fiona stepped back several paces from me. "Unlike most people here, we have been benefitted by and believe in sharing what we know to help others out."

"Let's go in. I can't wait to see my family; they're going to be so surprised to see me. My dad will be so excited to see me. I can't wait to talk to him." I stood but Fiona did not move out of the way.

"Taven. We can go in but before you do, you've got to understand something," she stood. She was almost as tall as I was. "You're dead."

"I know that," I said. She prevented my step around her.

"They're not going to be able to see you or us. They're not going to be able to hear you. We can go in, you can say your good byes, but this is just for you because it won't make a difference to them."

I nodded but didn't believe her. If I could use a mental crayon to travel through time and space, I could figure out a way to talk to my mom and dad. "So how do I get in? Should I wait for someone to come out, or go through an open window?"

"You were really left high and dry weren't you?" Fiona asked.

"What do you mean?" I responded.

"I could kind of understand you didn't know how to feel yourself from one place to another, but not knowing how to get inside a building without trailing behind someone else in the mortal world is criminal."

"Feel myself from one place... trailing behind someone else?"

"You don't even know what trailing is? You poor thing," she said, now looking at me as though I were the last little lonely puppy dog at the pet store.

"I guess my family wasn't thinking about what I really needed," I said.

"Exactly," she said.

I'd been so focused on Fiona and on getting inside the house, I'd forgotten we were not alone. Ben leaned against the house with a smirk on his face. Dan looked bored standing behind me in the middle of the lawn. "How do I get in?"

"I'll come with you. We will. For emotional support." She placed her hands on my shoulders again. "Keep feeling the picture of the house, un-focus so you move out of the mortal world, but focus on a room within your picture of the house. Once you've focused on that room, refocus on the mortal world. Got it?"

"What if the picture of the house I drew has a room that the real house doesn't have?" I asked, concerned about causing a rip in the inter-dimensional fabric.

"Just choose a room you are sure will be in the house," she said.

"How do you focus on more than one thing at a time?" I asked.

"You've just got to do it. You'll find it's not that hard, focusing on the mortal world and focusing on your picture are two very different things… like… like… walking and chewing gum, but they aren't that hard to do together."

"I'm not sure if I'm going to be able to keep everything I'm supposed to do straight. Can you walk me through while I'm doing it?" I asked.

"If you're concentrating on what I'm telling you, you're not going to be able to do it. Just remember. Picture the house, exit the mortal world, focus on a room in the house, refocus on the mortal world," she said.

Despite my fear that she must be getting sick of my inabilities, she maintained the sweet look of interest on her face. How could I give up with that kind of support? "Picture the house, exit world, focus on room, and re-enter world." She nodded.

Ben and Dan by this point had joined us once again, each with one hand on Fiona, like a miniature scrum, with me on one side and my three new friends on the other, although there was no rugby ball between us.

On closing my eyes, my picture of my house came back into view but no matter how hard I tried I could not summon an image of the inside of the house. I'd just been in a memory and seen the kitchen, but the concept of its appearance was always one step beyond my mental reach.

"Are you okay in there?" she asked.

"Yep," I lied. I gave up on chasing the memory and went with logic. There would surely be a kitchen in the house, but at that moment I remembered having relatives who cooked solely on their outdoor barbecue, and accordingly turned the kitchen into a recreation room with a fridge in it. Would that constitute a kitchen? Even a bathroom wasn't a sure thing. In the world I left, most bathrooms were indoors, but it wasn't that long ago that people used outhouses. My family had had an indoor bathroom, but what if the trauma of my death had caused them to convert their bathrooms into meditation spaces and move their bathroom to the backyard. But there had to be permit issues with that kind of thing. And bedrooms, what is a bedroom really?

"Any time now," Fiona whispered.

"Sorry," I said, determined to go with whatever first came to mind.

"Don't be sorry. Like I said before, the first time is always the hardest," she whispered.

I drew the house again in my mind, only this time, the picture sprung into place. I found it somewhat difficult to un-focus on the mortal world that I now could not see. I was a ten year-old all over again trying to get my genetically incapable tongue to roll.

"Is there a problem?" Fiona asked, causing the image to fade from view.

"Is it possible that my brain isn't capable of this? I can't un-focus without seeing the mortal world."

Fiona was now so close, I had to resist going cross-eyed. "That's your problem, Taven. You're stuck on the limitations of the body you used to have. You think the only way you can gather information or accomplish a task is by seeing, hearing, smelling, touching or tasting. It doesn't work that way here. Here you feel. Even the things you have been doing, walking, talking, you've been feeling them, not actually doing them. The reason you can do that much, is because even with a body, feeling is the way you get things done. Only with a body, your feelings are limited by the capacities of your body. No body. No capacities. Stop trying to do things, and focus on feeling them."

I nodded and my head came into contact with hers. Rather than pull back in pain, or be irritated by my bumbling, she smiled.

This new relationship was growing quite nicely in spite of the two weeds named Dan and Ben in our little flower patch.

I might as well have been learning how to use a tail or wings but if animal-kind could figure it out, so could I. I felt the house. I tried to inhale, the normal way I cleared my thoughts, but other than my chest rising, there was no rush of oxygen revitalizing my physical capacity. Don't do, feel. I stopped trying to inhale and went deep within myself. Beyond where I imagined my organs would have been, if my essence even had organs anymore, to the very core, the very essence of me. For an instant, it was as though I was amongst the particles composing my entity, the blackness of the canvas streaked by the ebb and flow of the building elements of me. Now independent of my surroundings, I felt myself leaving the mortal world.

The sublime experience of me was interrupted by the silly worries of present cares; I was now face to face with the decision of what room to get us into. I hastily chose and refocused on the idea of the mortal world. One reality faded into the other.

I was standing in the bathroom, next to the counter, which I hoped was mine but was not nearly so familiar as it should have been. Fiona stood still grasping my shoulders, beaming at me. Dan stood in the bathtub to her left, looking as though his freshly buttered toast had fallen face first onto the ground, while Ben, who was standing in the toilet, looked like a momma bear and I'd just taken her cub.

"You couldn't have picked another room?" he asked, stepping out of the toilet. "Maybe you need to spend some time in the john but I sure don't?"

"Calm down," she said, with enough of an edge that Ben might as well have seen the great hunter. Fiona instantly softened. "For his first time. It could have been a lot worse. We could have ended up in the plumbing."

I wasn't all that happy about the crowded conversation in a place not designed for crowds and wanted some confirmation we hadn't transported to some nether realm. "Is this my parent's house?"

"Take a look for yourself," Fiona answered, pointing to the window on the wall behind Ben, who glared at the floor.

I carefully shuffled past Ben to the small window. I looked down and saw the same well tended yard, the hedge and poplar tree. "It's the same house. So how do we get out of here? Ben looks like he's ready to pick a fight with the floor."

Fiona laughed. A genuine laugh. I couldn't help but notice she almost immediately put a stop to it with a not as genuine smile. "Just focus on the hallway on the other side of this door."

"Sure thing," I said as we again formed the human train. I started the process again, which was now natural. In an instant, we were in the hallway. Lining the walls down the corridor were pictures of people I did not know at all. "Who are they?"

"You don't know who these people are? Are you sure this is your parent's house?" asked Fiona

"I guess I wasn't sure. It seemed so familiar I just thought it was."

"There's probably a good explanation for why you felt like this was your house." Her hand was on my shoulder again. The electricity was now far more pleasing than uncomfortable. "Why don't you take us to where you think your parents are sleeping?"

Not really knowing which way was which, or which floor of the house we were on, I walked down the hallway, trailed by my three companions, until we reached another closed door. "This might be it," I said without the slightest idea of what was behind the door.

"If nothing else, I'm sure we'll figure out what's going on here. Get us in, and we can find out who's here," Fiona said, gripping my arm before finishing the sentence.

With very little effort we were on the other side. A large king-size bed was directly in front of us in the darkened room. The covers of the bed rose gently over the silhouette of the two people in it. I rushed to Mom's side of the bed, I strangely remembered she always liked to be closer to the door, even if only fractionally, because she liked to be the first one to get to us if something was wrong. I knelt down and looked into the face, which was not my mother's face.

I suppressed my initial angry reaction to what appeared to be my father's infidelity, I climbed over the bed to the other side, to look at his face. "This isn't my dad."

"Maybe your dad got plastic surgery?" laughed Ben in a low grumble.

"Taven, let's go outside for a minute," whispered Fiona, as she rubbed my arm.

"But I want to find my family," I whispered, but realizing the sleeping strangers wouldn't hear me anyway, I repeated more loudly, "I want to find my family."

"I'm sorry. They aren't here," she said.

This was the closest thing I had to home and I wasn't about to let it go. "Maybe they're on vacation."

"And they let the family staying here change the pictures on the wall. I don't know if you realized but this man's pictures were all over the hallway we just came from," she said again. "This isn't going to be easy for you to hear, but you've got to forget about your family. It's for the best."

"What do you mean 'forget about my family'? How could you say that?" I asked more sharply than I intended.

Fiona took my hand and led me out of the room. As angry as I was, I didn't resist her. "Do you even remember them?"

"I have memories of them." But at that moment those memories were out of reach and I wondered if I'd imagined them.

"I wasn't going to bring this up so early, but I can tell you need to know what's really going on here. Memories are skewed when a person comes here. People remember what they want to remember. What actually happened is lost in what people want to believe about themselves and about those around them."

"What?" I was stunned. Because the suggestion was outrageous and because I was struggling against believing it.

"Look, I'm not going to push this any further, but you need to realize that things aren't always the way we'd like them to be. Look at your relatives. How do you know your *father* is any different than the man who's shunned you because of your name? Or your mother. Is she any different than the woman who abandoned you as soon as she got what she wanted..."

"So what's the point then?" I interrupted. "If nothing's real, if everything that I was and am is fake, what's the point?"

"The point of what?" she asked.

"Existence!"

"Hasn't everything you've seen here shown you that the point of existence isn't so clear? Existence takes on whatever purpose you decide to assign to it."

"What's your purpose?"

I thought I saw her flinch, but she continued in the same calm manner as though she expected my question. "Being happy. Enjoying myself. Taking advantage of all of the amazing things this world's got to offer. Jump off a building. Soar through the air without a parachute. Run with the lions. Be with whoever, whenever I want. Feel good. Really feel good. With no consequences. That's what this is about. What else is there? You don't have to work anymore. You don't have to sustain life anymore. All that is left is finding happiness in whatever form it comes. Like I told you before, things are different here."

"But I miss my family. It doesn't feel good to be without them," I said.

"You couldn't be with the family you remember even if they did exist. Wouldn't you rather move on and enjoy what your new reality is?" she asked.

"I'm not ready to throw it all away, but if I did what would we do?"

"We would have some fun," she responded, her face now alive with anticipation.

"How are we supposed to do that?"

"Taven, I don't think it's coincidence you were drawn to this house. There's a very special little girl in this house. I don't know if you noticed her picture or not on the wall. Let's go back in." I arrived shortly after Fiona. Ben and Dan followed after. "Her." Fiona pointed to the picture of a young girl, who looked like she was about ten years old. She had blue eyes and chestnut-colored hair, a natural smile that I found myself smiling back at, and a natural beauty that held my attention. The image was familiar.

"What about her?" I asked.

"She's our ticket to fun," said Fiona.

"Our ticket to fun?" I asked.

"She's one in a million really. A very creative spirit, who when she sleeps creates a world where people like us, can really enjoy ourselves." Fiona caressed my cheek. Electricity accompanied her touch. "Want to feel the caress of my hand across your face? Want to taste your favorite food, want to have the adventure you've always dreamed of having, want to feel like you are alive? Then this very special girl is your ticket."

"Is it going to hurt her in any way?" I asked.

"Of course not. Trust me. It will be worth it." She turned away from me and crept along the hallway. Coming to a door, she disappeared for a brief instant then reappeared. "She's here. Come with me. Hold on."

I grabbed her shoulder and was drawn into the little girl's room. Covers tucked under her chin, head laying to the side, soft features and porcelain skin, long brown hair spread across the pillow, she slept peacefully. I was mesmerized by her. I didn't notice anything else about the room. "What's her name?"

"It's... Becky," Fiona responded.

"Becky," I repeated, feeling a connection with this little girl.

I don't know if Fiona grabbed my head and jerked towards her or not, but I was face to face with her. I saw a passion in her eyes that thrilled and frightened me. "All you need to do is put your hands on either side of her head and concentrate on joining her. But do it with your mind. Don't try and jam your head into hers. Feel it," she said stooping over the bed.

"Am I that predictable?" I asked, as I remembered the embarrassing runner incident.

"It's a common thing. Don't worry about it." Fiona placed her hand on my shoulder. Dan and Ben joined in behind her. "Just put your hands on either side of her head and I'll take care of the rest."

"Is this going to hurt her?" I repeated.

"Of course not. Like I said, this is a special little girl, an open-minded girl. She'll be fine. We've been doing this a long time," she said.

"Okay." I placed my hands on either side of Becky's little head and concentrated on her, I saw Fiona slip her hands under my hands as everything faded from view.

I can feel my fingers

Light and matter whizzing around, by and through me, I sensed she was also present. I called out to her, "Fiona, are you there?"

Her bodiless voice whispered, "Yes."

"Where are we?" I asked.

"Somewhere between where we were and where we are going."

"Where are Ben and Dan?"

"We're here too," a grizzly voice grumbled.

"So where are we going? What's happening?" I asked.

"You'll see."

The next thing I knew I was standing in front of a large brick house, its windows and doors accented by white washed wood. Providing a covering for the front entrance, a balcony, supported by ten ornately carved pillars, stretched the length of the house. A long row of bushes, standing like sentinels, led from the head of the path where I stood to the entrance. The well-tended lawn extended to a wall that stood at the edge of my field of vision in every direction. Wisps of grayish white clouds illuminated by the light of the full moon passed over. Countless stars shone down speaking of their majesty and my own insignificance in one breath. I could hear the grass beneath my feet and stomped for the satisfaction of actually having an impact on the environment in which I was placed. Reaching down, I grabbed a twig and snapped it. But more breath taking than anything I saw or heard or felt was that I felt alive again.

I only then realized that Fiona, and only Fiona, stood next to me, her cheeks colored with a natural blush, her lips a blazing red, the mystery of her green eyes irresistible. Strands of her blond hair danced behind her in the wind. I felt her fingers tighten around my wrist as she turned to look at me, her eyes filled with excitement.

"Do you see?" she asked me.

"You... you're... umm... you look good," I stammered.

"You're not too bad yourself," she replied.

I looked down. I pinched my clothing and could both feel and manipulate the fabric. I could feel my fingers slide along the surface. I rubbed my hands against my cheeks and could feel the light stubble just beneath the surface of the skin on my chin. "I'm alive," I cried, much too much like a mad scientist.

"Yes, you are," she said. Twisting a lock of her hair around one of her fingers. She bit her bottom lip lightly, drew her mouth into a playful smile and asked, "Did I mention that I like you?"

I felt my face flush but before I could allow myself to be carried away by the currents of romance, my old vending cart flashed into memory. First the sausage went on the grill, then into the bun, then the condiments, ketchup before mustard, onions before relish, then into the paper sleeve.

"Is something wrong?"

Unable to force the visions of hot dog vending from my mind, I smiled and said, "I can't stop thinking about hot dogs."

"That's kind of weird," she said, "but not really. Lots of people get pretty excited about the prospect of getting something to eat. But I've got something better in mind for us."

Before I could say, "What's that?" she pivoted in front of me and put her arms around my waist, close enough that although our faces weren't touching, I could feel the warmth of her skin.

"I think you can guess."

I gulped. "So where are we?"

"Do you remember what I told you about Becky being a very special girl?"

"Uh huh."

"The reason she's so special is that when we are in her dreams, we are alive."

"Dreams?" I clenched my fist and could feel my nails dig into my palm. This was against one of the few pieces advice I had received. I opened my fingers and could feel the flow of blood. "How?"

"I guess I could explain this all to you right now but," she said running her finger across my cheek. "we've only got so much time before she wakes up. And I've got something I really want to show you."

"Me?" I asked.

She nodded and started walking up the foliage-lined path without waiting for me. Once at the steps leading to the front door, she stopped and motioned for me to follow. I tried to brush away the anxiety I felt for being in the dream.

"Are you okay?" she asked.

"I'm fine," I said as I tried to break the chain of thoughts. I walked to her.

She took my hand and led me to the front door. Without ringing the doorbell or otherwise announcing her entrance, she opened the door. A long hallway, flanked by openings whose light spilled into the dark passageway lighting it somewhat, stretched before us. Midway down the corridor was a flight of steps, which led up to darkness.

"Come on," she said as she tightened her grip on my wrist. She quickened her pace. "There's a bedroom upstairs all ready for us. We're going to have a lot of fun, you and I."

"Shouldn't we get to know each other better first? This seems to be moving a little fast, although I am grateful you saved me and all."

"Why are you so hesitant? Don't you like the way I look? I can change if you need..." she asked.

"I do," I said. "I just feel uncomfortable."

Unmoved, she said, "Let's go work on making you comfortable."

I walked with her, not wanting to be there, but allowing my curiosity to take me. The closer we got the more the excitement of what was to come dispelled the shadows of doubt.

But that all changed the moment I looked into one of the rooms that lined the hallway and saw a girl standing alone weeping. Every allure she had, any desire to follow her, to be with her, was extinguished. "We should check on that girl," I said.

"She'll be fine. Don't worry about it," Fiona responded.

"She doesn't look fine, she's crying," I said. "Doesn't it bother you that there's a little girl crying in that room over there?

"Remember this is just a dream. It doesn't matter. She's probably not even real."

"Do you know for sure?" I asked.

"Look. You came here to be with me," she said.

"You know, I'm not even sure why I came in here. You brought me. You've really helped me but it doesn't feel right not to check on this girl."

"This is a dream. If we don't take advantage of this time, it's gonna be gone."

Her hair continued to dance around her as though gently tossed by the wind despite the fact we were inside the house. Every positive detail enhanced, every negative detail minimized, it was like she was the end product of a photo shoot, absolutely alluring, but not so alluring that I could take the risk the little girl was only imaginary.

A scream pierced the air and left all in silence besides a guttural and deep bubbling sound, like the sound an evil fish tank cleaner would make. I stepped away from Fiona and towards the door.

"Come with me," I said to Fiona, but as I took a step away, I felt the blood rush back into my hand. She was gone. Her finger marks were still clearly visible on my wrist.

I walked into the room, deviating neither to the left nor right. "Are you okay?"

There was no response. As I came closer to her, I recognized that it was Becky. The closer I got, the more afraid she seemed. "It's okay I won't hurt you."

She cowered until she sat with her arms around her knees, her ankle length blue flowered nightgown stretched around her legs. I walked to her and knelt down. "I'm here to help you. Is there something wrong?"

Those big blue watery eyes never left the opposite corner of the room.

I said, "Hey. Don't worry. It's just a dream you have nothing to worry about..."

I don't know whether I heard her scream or felt the impact of what seemed to be a wrecking ball first. My unscheduled flight was stopped by a unforgivingly solid wall. When I hit the ground I instinctively searched for the injuries attached to the pain I felt but found my limbs worked as they should.

Standing in front of Becky was what I could best describe as a man-sized crustacean, fresh from some radioactive salt-water sludge pit that had transformed the shrimp into a monstrosity. Red as a strawberry from head, which was more pimple-size than head-size, to toe, it had an armor-like shell which was knobbed and blackened at the tips. Its claws on both primary limbs, about ten times the size of its head, flinched and creaked. Vile gurgling echoed in my ears, as did Becky's sobbing. A raised gigantic claw hung ominously over her.

Casting out all thought of self-preservation, I shouted, "Leave her alone."

Turning its attention to me, the monster responded with the same low gurgling noise I'd heard before.

I jumped, and to my surprise, bridged the great distance between us, and lineman-like buried my shoulder into its midsection. Having expected to knock the thing over, my courage somewhat faltered when I bounced off of it, the only evidence I had made contact with it being the amused gurgle. I, on the other hand, had what I was sure were bruises on the side of my face and my shoulder from those unforgiving nodules covering its entire shell.

The monster made no attempt to harm me. Instead it turned again towards Becky and snapped its claws at her face, the force of the snap whipping her hair behind her. She opened her mouth but her fear was muted.

At that moment my favorite scene from my favorite Kung-Fu movie came to mind. In that scene, when defeat was almost certain, the hero leapt high into the air, and with great speed flew foot first into the face of the villain, effecting a great victory. As a third grader, on the verge of being pummeled by another third grader who was the size of a sixth grader, I had attempted this move but was disappointed to learn two fundamental facts. The first was that I had neither sufficient vertical leap nor hang time to get my foot to his face. The second was that I was not as flexible as my hero. Ripped pants and pulled groin, I lay defeated as my third grade nemesis stood over me.

But I was out of options. I needed a plan and this was a plan. I leapt and, to my astonishment, I hung in the air at about twice the height of the crustacean. I pointed all four of my limbs at the creature, balled my hands into fists, bent my left leg bent and extended my right, the leg that would make contact. My groin felt fine and I knew my pants were not ripped because there was no draft where there should be no draft. Body properly positioned, I jolted to commence movement and careened towards the beast, speed far exceeding that caused by gravity, and in a moment, kicked the side of its knee and knocked it completely out of joint.

A shriek, like the one a lobster makes when it is put in hot water, escaped the beast.

"Looks like we're having lobster tonight, Becky," I shouted. If she smiled, terror so quickly robbed her of the source of it that it may as well never have been there.

Using its left claw as a make shift crutch, dragging the lame leg behind it, the mutated crustacean approached me and, far more quickly than I anticipated, swung a gigantic claw at my face. I ducked, but not fast enough to avoid the hard shell scraping along the top of my head.

Not only was it like dragging rusty nails across my scalp but male pattern baldness ran in my family; I could accept that but I was not okay with balding happening prematurely, especially as a result of an oversized appetizer taking a swipe at me.

My primary advantage being agility, I ran toward the back of the beast, hoping I would be able to figure out my next move while it drug behind. Stupidly, I forgot the crustacean creature was more interested in Becky, and the moment I was out of view, it inched towards her, all the more menacing because of its limp. Not having time for another might leap, I drove my fist into the back of its leg, its leg buckling under the force of my blow.

Those massive legs could no longer support the oversized torso of the creature. It stumbled backwards and fell where I had been. I sprung its chest. The warm spray from its hiss, showered my face.

"All we need is a little butter." No sooner had I looked up to gauge Becky's response than the thing disappeared and I dropped to the floor I turned to the little girl. "We did it, Becky."

She looked to the ground.

I walked over to her. "You've got nothing to worry about. I know you really wanted to eat some of that lobster. I know. I can see it in your face. It looked so tasty didn't it?"

"But I don't like lobster..." she said.

"Maybe it was a good thing he disappeared then. Did you see how I took care of that guy no problem?" I reached down to help her up but she resisted. Whatever comfort I had given her had been violently taken from her. "Why are you crying? I'm here and it's gone. You can stop crying now. Really, you can stop. That guy is gone and this is only a dream..."

"Look out!" she screamed.

Heavily muscled human-like arms and legs, a leather tunic over its chest and upper legs, covered from head to toe with fur the color of a raven, crouched, its lion-like eyes and mouth gaping, yellowish teeth the size of steak knives, the abomination roared. If ever there was a sound that would make someone want to run away at the hearing of it, this was the sound.

"Get back," I yelled to Becky, but my voice seemed lost in the echo of the intensity of the sound. She stood but seemed to be unable to move any faster than in slow motion. A flash in my peripheral vision, I ducked, barely avoiding the blunt force of a massive clawed hand across my face, but not avoiding the cheese grater like drag across my scalp.

I scrambled to my feet and threw my fist with all the force I could muster. The creature recoiled as my clenched hand found a gap in its tunic and penetrated its side. As I drew my hand back, I was surprised; it looked and weighed more like a bowling ball than a hand. Not pretty, but I figured a numb and swollen hand was at least a weapon. I swung again. As its teeth pierced my flesh, I discovered my hand was not the cudgel I'd imagined it to be.

Rag doll like, it whipped me around like a dog wrestling over a shoe with its owner. Every moment I expected my joints to come unhinged or my hand, which was clamped between his jaws, to dislocate and tear my arm off. I kicked frantically but found no target that caused a loosening of its grip. I might not have much hope, but I was a distraction. "Becky... Becky! Get out of here!"

"I can't. I'm stuck."

I tried to see her but I was flailing too wildly to focus on one spot. "Can you get out?"

"No, I'm stuck. Help me! Watch out!"

Everything visually was now a blur but I knew what was happening, I was going to be used as a weapon on the little girl. She couldn't move and I was going to be used to wipe her out. A particularly fearsome jerk whipped me out of my worries and up towards the head. I held my left arm out straight. The force of the swing drove my knife-like fingers into its eye, which was enough to get it to release its grip.

While it whimpered and pawed at its damaged eye, I ignored what I was sure was a permanently mangled hand and looked to Becky, her feet planted beneath the floorboards. "How did that happen?"

"I just sunk in. Are you okay?"

"I will be soon." Despite the intensity of what had occurred, I felt no pain and did not experience any restriction in movement. Facing the distracted creature, I threw my again bowling ball sized hand, it seemed to swell the instant I decided to strike, into its side. It howled, folding nearly in two. I grabbed its ears and drove its face into the floor. It lay motionless. The creature vanished. "Everything's going to be…"

Immediately, a rumble in the floorboards lifted me off the ground, as though something very heavy had been dropped at a distant point and its ripple was only now reaching me. A rhythmic pounding continued until a creature constructed of rough stones, many times larger than either the crustacean or the cat, crashed through the doorway. Its head, if you could call it that, always sat atop a large stone that rolled freely and in every direction, with a long line of rocks, as though they'd been shoved into a transparent and flexible tube, hanging from either side of the large stone. It moved as the large center stone rolled. Its voice, which came not from a mouth or vocal cords, but rather the grinding of its head with its stone body, echoed, "Give me the girl."

"Leave her alone. Just let us go."

"No," the floorboards groaned as it rolled towards me. Before I could come up with an attack plan, the end of one of its long rock chains, I guess it was its arm, smashed on the ground next to me, its rock fist crashing through the floor exposing the lighted basement below.

Before that arm was lifted from the ground, its other arm cracked like a whip, the reach of it coming within a hair of my nose. Caught off guard, I didn't notice the huge body of the beast hurtling through the air directly towards me; a direct impact was inevitable. I closed my eyes and waited as Becky's screams echoed in my ears.

I landed on my butt on the floor of Becky's room. Fiona, Ben and Dan watched me with what seemed like an amused look on their faces. "What were you doing in there?" Fiona asked. "If I knew you had a superhero fantasy, I would have set things up differently. I just figured since you're a boy and I'm a girl we could... fulfill one of mine"

"What happened to the little girl?" I asked.

"Look at the bed," said Fiona. Becky was asleep. "You got caught up in a little girl's nightmare. Nightmare's build character."

"I couldn't just leave her there," I said sheepishly.

"That's what Ben and Dan were there for." Fiona explained.

"I didn't see them in there helping her."

Fiona moved over to the edge of the bed and sat on it. She motioned for me to do the same. "We're not there to interfere in dreams. In fact, we don't want to interfere at all. It would ruin her if we did. All we want is to be able to enjoy the landscape of her dreams. Like I said, she's a special girl. If we interfere, we ruin her."

If I had a body my face would have been beet red. Guilt burned within me. "I ruined her?"

Fiona grabbed my hand and pulled me next to her. "No, I don't think so. You may have delayed the natural course of the dream but you didn't change it."

"No, you didn't," spat Ben. "That girl would have done better on her own."

"Why didn't you guys help me?"

Fiona answered for them. "If they did they would ruin her. You've got to let nightmares run their course. Ben and Dan were there to make sure you and I didn't interfere with the dreams this special little girl."

"You're telling me she's the one who came up with those... things." I instinctively looked at my hand, which looked like it always did.

"Yes. Another example of why we ought to simply look out for ourselves. You don't know what's lurking beneath the surface," Fiona said. "Being in dreams is a lot like being in a big city. There are some great places to go and some not so great places to go. There are some exciting things to do and some stupid things to do. Try not to do anything stupid next time, okay? I like you. I'd like for you to stay in one piece."

Fiona patted my leg. The electricity of her touch, which I think was as intense as it had been before, was irrelevant in comparison to what I had experienced in the dream when she touched me. She stood and motioned to Ben and Dan. "Meet us back here tonight. Just focus on this bedroom like we showed you."

"Where are you going?" I asked.

"Giving you some time to figure things out," she answered. "Like I said, you've got to look out for yourself and what you want. If you figure out if I'm what you want, meet me back here. My offer is definitely still on the table."

Ben and Dan vanished from sight. Fiona whispered, "I'm on your side. Don't forget that, okay?" She disappeared leaving no tangible evidence she had left the room, not even a rustle of the window coverings.

I looked down at Becky's tiny face, much more peaceful than she had been in the dream. Fiona was right, no real harm had been done to Becky. She'd wake up and probably not remember a thing.

Stepping away from the bed, I drew a mental picture of the clearing where I'd begun my journey. I didn't have anyone or anything there, but I knew it was the right place to go. No reasons, I just knew. I'd go there, gather my thoughts, purge myself of old ways of thinking and settle into this new reality with a woman who seemed genuinely interested in me.

My connection to Sherwood Forest

It seemed like it was always autumn in this field - it was fitting really. Everything was shaded with the bronzes and yellows of faded pictures from an old photo album, it was a realm where uncomfortable nostalgia reigned. I noticed it more after my experience in the dream. There I was an actor in the play, here I was a spectator.

I focused.

It wasn't dawn yet in the mortal world; no one was in the park. I'm not sure it would have made a difference if someone was there, but the feeling that I was really missing something, that I was alone grew. It wasn't that I needed company, at least I didn't think I needed a companion, it was more that. Being in the dream, really feeling again, made me realize that in death I was missing something so intimately related with my experience with existence: my body.

I released my focus and returned to my quiet reality. My choice between Fiona and Becky played again and again in my mind. As good as it felt to be in the dream, as wanted as I apparently was by Fiona, I couldn't shake the idea that by making a choice other than the one I did I would have been betraying them both. But that was just a thought with no legs to carry it to justification. I craved being in the dream again. Maybe moving forward with my existence, finding happiness needed to come ahead of nagging worries. I didn't know what the future held with Fiona but at least it was an option. Everything else about me seemed fixed in the past. A memory forced itself on me.

"Taven, you are seventeen years old. You're going to be going to university next year and you need to earn some money to do it," my dad had said.

"But Dad, I don't want to work at a burger place or the supermarket. I'm probably going to be working in an office for the rest of my life. I don't want to be inside," I had responded.

"You could apply at the city. Work for the maintenance crew," Mom had offered.

"My friend Evan worked for the city and he barely made minimum wage. He said he was bored most of the time, standing around watching someone else do work," I had reasoned.

"I've got a client who is looking to sell his son's hot dog cart. You'd have to be motivated but you would be able to choose your own hours and if you were smart you'd probably make more money in less time than your friends once you got things going. But it would be hard work up front," Dad had said.

I was back in the clearing. I remembered that Mom and Dad had purchased the cart for me. In spite of all the struggles with money, they had given me the opportunity to excel. If only I could see them, talk to them, ask them what they think... I shook my head and said aloud. "The rules have changed, it's time for me to move on."

I stared at the untouchable blades of grass in the space between my crossed legs. A faint scratching sound, like nails on sandpaper, drew my attention across the field. Clinging to the side of a tree was a large squirrel. It wouldn't have been strange to see a squirrel in the park, but this was the first animal I'd come across in this hazy otherworld. It looked directly at me, climbed down to the base and scurried to a tree closer to where I sat. I asked, "Got any advice for a guy who doesn't know whether he's coming or going?"

The large squirrel leapt from the tree and approached by a zigzagged path, one typical of squirrels, at least I seemed to know it was typical. He at last stopped on my leg and, standing on his hind legs, pointed his large brown nose in my direction. It seemed to me as though he was waiting for something. "So, any advice for me?" I asked.

He scrambled up my shirt and onto my shoulder. As he placed his clawed front paw gently on my cheek, I found myself transported to a tall tree, its green leaves rustling as though dancing in the wind, great branches reaching up all around me into the sky, which sparkled with thousands upon thousands of visible stars. Riding along one of the branches as though it was a roller coaster, up and down, around and over, I came to the edge and looked to the field below. I was in my park, although things seemed so much newer. No rust on the slide and the swings swayed without screeching in the blowing wind.

Despite the principle source of light being the moon, I could see to the trees bordering the river on the other side of the park. On the ground below me, a group of boys, dressed in pants that were cropped with what looked like an elastic at the knee and wearing boots that rose to the ankle and striped shirts with collars that made them look like sailors, were pointing at me.

"I bet you can't hit that squirrel," one of them shouted.

"I bet you I can," responded the boy with his arm cocked behind him.

He flung a stone towards me. I must have been hit, because my field of vision left the ground and rose to the stars, which seemed to flee ever so slightly from me as I fell to the ground. Four heads intruded into what I knew were my last glimpses of the night sky. I watched the transformation from youthful mischievousness to faces wrenched with the terror of irreparable consequence.

"Don't be dead. I didn't mean to kill you, honest. I didn't think I'd hit you," the boy who had been more deadly than he ever intended said, while poking me with a stick.

"Let's get out of here," shouted one of the other boys, causing all four heads to disappear from my view, leaving me alone, as tree and starry sky dissolved into blackness.

The memory complete, I was back in my field, seated on the ground with this squirrel on my shoulder. The recklessness and finality of what I had seen confirmed everything Fiona had said to me; trust no one but yourself and get what makes you happy. It couldn't have been coincidence that I came across this squirrel, could it? My problem was rather than illumination, emptiness accompanied this discovery, which hung as an almost unbearable, but irremovable, weight about my neck. "I figure out what existence really is about and I feel worse. Is that what I have to look forward to?"

The squirrel leapt from my shoulder to my lap. It seemed to shake its head, but said nothing.

"So you know enough to know I'm wrong but can't tell me? What is going on?" I hoped the squirrel would at least take me into another memory, but it only sat and stared. "Was that you in the dream?"

It nodded but said nothing.

"Is there a point to life?"

"Yep."

I nearly fell backwards. I knew enough to know squirrels don't usually talk. I hadn't seen his mouth move but I definitely heard a voice. I quickly shooed the thought the squirrel wasn't the best thing to ask for advice and asked, "What am supposed to do here?"

"You're not going to figure it out talking to the squirrel like that, Taven," said the voice.

I looked over my shoulder and saw green tights covering the knees directly behind me. I scrambled to my feet to face the person while the squirrel casually bounded back to the tree. The man was dressed as though he'd come right out of the Sherwood Forest portrayed in movies. Green vest, green shorts, three-sided hat with a canary yellow feather on the side. He was dressed to rescue. He had a bright clear face; his eyes shone with excitement and life, like a two-year old that knows what he is about to do is going to be an awful lot of fun.

"How do you know my name?" I asked.

"I know a lot of things," he said.

I could tell by the look on his face this was a game he had been looking forward to for a very long time. "Are you celebrating Halloween? Kind of ironic really considering we're dead and the whole holiday is about ghosts..."

He laughed. "Very funny. What are you dressed as? A mortician?"

I looked down and I was suddenly dressed from head to toe in black. "How did you do that?"

"Do what?"

"This," I said motioning to the macabre outfit. "This awful thing"

"You chose that yourself," he laughed.

"No, I didn't I wasn't wearing black when I got here."

"Who said you were wearing black?"

I looked down. I was back in my normal clothes.

"I expect you're also jealous because you don't have the physique to pull off this kind of outfit." He tugged on one of his lapels.

"Look. It's nice to know there are crazy dead people, but I'm really busy. So feel free to…" Before I was finished he was gone.

"It sure seems like you're busy," said a voice. "Feeling sorry for yourself while you count the blades of grass between your legs is very important work that must take precedence over me."

I turned to face him. He was about a soccer field away, but I could hear him as though he was next to me. "Who are you and what do you want from me?"

"Come over here and I'll tell you."

This game felt old before it started but at least I was talking to someone. It was better than being alone. Lame or not, if I was going to play, I was going to play. Thanks to Fiona's guidance, I knew if I drew the spot in my mind, I'd be drawn to it. So I did, and the moment I was finished, I was there. However, by the time I was there, he was not. I turned around and he was back in the spot where we began.

Drawing that spot, by the time I got to where he was, he was back in the spot I'd just left. We continued this strange sort of dance for what seemed like the amount of time something this monotonous would interest a toddler until an idea struck me. Rather than move, I only closed my eyes and before I knew it, jolly green happy boy was at my side looking absolutely engaged.

"That was awesome. You totally tricked me." And then he laughed; the kind of laugh that wasn't inspired by cruelty, hurt or mocking, but the offspring of pure enjoyment. "Do you want to do it again? This time I'll chase you. Okay?"

"Hold on. Like you said, I'm very busy. I've got a really important thing I've got to do tonight and I've got to be sure I'm ready to do it," I said.

"What are you doing that's so important?" he asked.

"What does it matter to you? I don't even know who you are?"

"Yes, you do."

"No, I don't. I've never seen you before in my life."

"Yes, you have," he sang, his eyes lighting with anticipation.

"No, I haven't," I sang back.

"Yes, you have."

I exhaled and gritted my teeth. "Who are you?"

"You've got to guess."

"How am I supposed to guess? There were six billion people on earth when I was alive. I suppose there have been billions of people that have lived on the earth before I was alive. How am I supposed to know which of those billions of people you happen to be?"

"I'll give you three tries, then I'll give you a clue."

"Three tries to figure out who you are amongst billions?"

"Yep. And a clue," he said as though the words tasted like the most delicious desert as they left his mouth.

"Will you leave me alone if I guess?" I asked.

He nodded.

"Umm. Robin Hood?" I asked.

"You wish. No way, two more," he sang.

"Julius Caesar?" I asked.

"No. Do I look Roman to you?" The instant he said it, a laurel wreath sat on his head. With deep emotion and pronounced overacting, he asked "Et tu, Brute?" laughed, then said. "One more."

"Don Quixote. That's got to be it. You're crazy and so was he."

"I'm not the crazy one. Not speaking Spanish. Windmills are windmills, not giants. I know who I am. You're the one who doesn't. You're the crazy one," he said and let out what must have been a victory shout.

"Well?" I asked.

"Well what?" he said.

"What do you mean well what? So what's my clue?" I asked.

"You've got to say sorry first," he sang, holding the word first in a falsetto voice.

I couldn't take any more of this; I drew and went to a tree on the other side of the clearing. And there he was next to me. "Do you want to play this game again?"

"No. I want you to stop bugging me. Okay?" I said, wishing I had some way of restraining this fool.

"Okay. Do you want your clue?" he asked.

"Fine. What's the clue?" I said.

"You are older than me." He said it as though this statement would open a whole new world of understanding for me.

It didn't. "Okay, that means that you could be any of the billions that were born after I was born. Not too helpful."

"You at least need to guess. If you guess, I'll give you another clue," he sang again.

I had no idea, so I made up a name. "Bilfur Snooglegrass."

The man howled. "You're so funny. That's a funny name. Snooglegrass. But it's not the right one. Okay. Next clue. We are from the same town."

Now I was interested. He could be someone I actually knew. A stream of faces passed before my eyes. I had to assume they were from my town, although aside from knowing I was from a town and what it basically looked like, I had no idea what it was called or where it was located. There was the boy who fell down drunk behind the back tire of a truck and had his head run over, but he survived. A fifteen-year-old girl died in a car accident, but this guy was no girl. Every name I thought of, every tragedy I scanned, added to the weight that pressed itself on my heart. Life was unfair and death wasn't any better. Refusing to increase my burden by thinking about any more untimely deaths, I stopped thinking about it. "I'm not trying to be rude, but I really don't know who you are. This was a lot of fun, but I've got to get ready for tonight."

"Come on, just guess. It's a good surprise," he said, unfazed by my downpour on his picnic.

"I ... don't... know. I don't even remember my own life. I don't remember what my house looks like. I don't remember where it is. Last night I went into a house I thought was mine only to find out it wasn't. I don't remember my life outside of my stupid vending cart and... and... what does it matter to you. I don't feel like playing games right now. I don't want to hurt your feelings but I'm just not in the mood for this."

"But you know me," he whispered, no longer jovial.

His solemnity pierced my stony exterior and old and powerful emotions rushed through me. I was in my grade six self, and the school year was almost over. I was in the second last period of the day when I was called to go to the office. The vice principal told me my grandparents were going to come for my sister and I. I asked why, but they said that Grandma and Grandpa would tell us when they arrived. Based on the vice principal's serious approach, I assumed the worst was about to happen. I wondered what I'd done for Grandma and Grandpa to pick me up at school. But they weren't only coming for me, they were getting my sister Karen too.

Sitting on a hard wooden bench facing the secretaries who sat in front of the offices of the principal and the vice principals, I agonized in the unknown. Was Mom sick? Did Dad lose his job? Were we moving to a new town? Were we both getting kicked out of school? It seemed like forever before Karen joined me, at least now I had someone to bounce my insecurities off of. "How come Grandma and Grandpa are picking us up?"

"I think it's for a special treat. 'member how they went to Hawaii and just got back?" my sister, then in grade two, responded.

"Yah, I do," I said.

"Well. They're probably going to surprise us with an awesome present," she said, her face telling the story.

"You think so?" I asked, willing my sagging heart to lift.

"Yep. What else could it be?"

Her hope was enough to make the next period of silence bearable. When Grandma and Grandpa arrived, they didn't say much but they squeezed us tight and carried Karen out to the car, which I thought was weird, but I went with it. Grandpa had picked me up, but I could tell I was a little bit too heavy for him. I hadn't been carried in a while, and it's nice to be babied from time to time, but I also didn't want to break my grandpa. They silently belted us into the car and pulled out of the school parking lot.

"Grandma, when do we get the present from Hawaii?" I asked.

Grandma White bowed her head, and I could hear her gasping as though she couldn't get enough air. Grandpa put his hand on her back.

"It's okay if you didn't get us a present. We're just happy to see you and get out of school," Karen said. I was put out and a little frustrated that we wouldn't be getting a present.

"It's not about that sweetheart," Grandma responded. My heart leapt. We were going to get a present. "John, pull the car over. Right there by that park."

"Okay," Grandpa said, his voice trembling.

"We're going to the park? Yahoo!" I yelled. But now Karen was quiet.

Grandpa parked the car. To get to the park, we had to cross the bridge that went over the river. I wasn't too bothered by how quiet everyone was as we walked; I was enthralled by the sound of the river as it passed, the birds chirping in the trees and the play park with swings and a slide that stood near the center of the field. Having grabbed a handful of rocks, I tossed them into the river as we crossed.

Having crossed the bridge, Grandpa and Grandma, Grandpa holding my hand and Grandma holding Karen's hand, led us to some benches off to the side of the clearing.

"Can we go to the park now?" I asked as we veered away from it.

"Not now, Taven, we need to talk to you about something," Grandma whispered, tears now streaming down her cheeks.

"Can we have our present then?" I asked.

"Taven! Stop." Grandpa had never snapped at me before, but it was enough to make me stop.

"John, he doesn't know," Grandma said.

"I'm sorry, Taven. Come sit on my knee." I sat on his knee and saw Grandma pull Karen close into her arms. Karen was crying and I wondered what I was missing. "You guys, your mommy and your little brother were in a car accident this morning." My chest felt like it might tear in two. The ceiling of my world was beginning to crumble and yet Grandpa went on. "Your mommy was driving through an intersection when a truck hit the back corner of your van."

"Did our van get broked?" I asked.

"Taven. Your mommy is in the hospital. She's very hurt but the doctor said she's going to be alright. But…" Grandpa paused for a very long time. The world seemed to stop, every sound, every movement, as if everything waited for Grandpa to continue. "… but your baby brother died in the accident."

I felt Grandpa's body throb as he held me tightly.

"But when is he going to come home?" Karen asked.

"He's not coming home," Grandma sighed, not in a frustrated way but as though the sadness just forced its way out. "He's... he's... in heaven."

It was then that it hit me that I wouldn't see my two year old brother toddle into my bedroom again, first thing in the morning, to smack my face, smile and wake me up. "Hungy." That was the way he asked for breakfast. I wouldn't hear him say the word. I wouldn't hear his giggle. My mind raced to the last time I saw him. He was in my mother's arms in his one-piece pajama suit, smiling and his pudgy hand twisting at the wrist. I wouldn't see that again. Life felt like it couldn't go on. I felt numb.

"Where's Dad?" I asked.

"He's with your mom at the hospital. He's going to come as soon as he can but you guys are going to stay with us for a little while," Grandpa answered.

"But who's with my brother?" I asked.

"I'm sure great grandma Mercy's taking care of him," Grandma answered.

"And Auntie Sophie," Grandpa added.

"Can you call them on the phone to make sure," Karen said, through hiccoughs of grief.

"Oh sweetheart," said Grandma as she pulled Karen in closer. No one spoke for a while. "I'll pray to God tonight, to ask Him to make sure."

"Me too grandma. He listens to kids' prayers the most," Karen responded resolutely.

It helped to know that Grandma thought there was something we could do to help him. That hope took the edge off of the realization that life without my little brother was not going to be the same, and never would be. There was life before Finn, but I couldn't imagine there being life without him.

We never did play at the park that day. I wondered, at the time, whether I'd ever want to play at a park again. But I did. Though derailed for a time, life got back on its tracks almost naturally. Sure, there were a lot of people who helped and comforted and consoled, but in the end, life simply moved on and we moved with it.

After a short stay at Grandma and Grandpa's, with Dad visiting us every night, when Mom was well enough to leave the hospital, we returned home and before long we were all back in a normal routine.

"Finn?" I asked, hardly believing the man standing in front of me could be that little brother I'd lost so long ago.

"How did you guess? You were so far off before, I figured we would be here for two weeks before you figured it out," he said, clearly impressed.

"Is it really you?" I asked. It was like losing ten dollars, resigning myself to the fact the money was lost forever, and then out of the blue someone returning it at the very moment I needed it, times ten thousand.

"Uh huh. I already told you it's me. Are you surprised?" he beamed.

I grabbed Finn's shoulders then drew him into my chest. "I thought I'd never get to see you again. How did you get so big?"

Finn returned my embrace, and as he did, a warmth engulfed me. "When I got here I was big and I could do all the things I had been thinking but couldn't do before."

My thoughts turned to Karen's prayer. "Did great grandma Mercy and Auntie Sophie take care of you?"

"How did you know? They're so nice. Always checking up on me," he said.

"I've been looking for Mom and Dad. I never thought I'd find you in the process. This is... this is... what heaven must feel like," I said.

"I missed you too, big brother."

Moments ago he was running around acting like a maniac, and now he was possessed of a serenity and certainty that I had never before seen. I patted his back, stepped away from him and sat down. I motioned for him to sit next to me, which he did. "So what have you been doing all this time?"

"Helping people. Helping family. I look for members in our family that need special help and I find them and I help them." I wondered to myself how a boy who had no more than two years' experience in life could be qualified to help people out. As if sensing my doubt, he continued, "Just because I didn't get to do all the things with my body that everyone else gets to do, doesn't mean I don't know how to do things. Doesn't mean I can't tell when someone's lost or hurt or struggling. And doesn't mean that I can't help out."

It sounded as though I wasn't the first person with whom he was having this conversation, but I was curious, so I asked, "How do you know what to do?"

"What makes you so sure the time we were alive was the only time we were learning and being?" he responded.

"What do you mean?" I asked.

"Does the fact that you can't remember a thing mean that it never happened? Like, the fact that you couldn't remember who I am, does that mean I don't exist?" he asked.

"Of course not," I said.

"I don't remember learning how to help people, but that doesn't mean that I didn't learn sometime. If not when I was alive, then it must have been sometime," he paused for a few seconds to let the idea sink in, but offered no further explanation. "Let's go to the river."

Side by side, my brother and I followed the meandering path through the park toward downtown until we came to the opening in the trees that led to the river. The same place I had spent some underwater quality time. My mind swirled with the questions I wanted to ask him, but somehow silence seemed to be the best way to enjoy his company. He took in the world around him as though he was seeing it for the first time, not surprised, but clearly in awe.

We walked up to the riverbank, where Finn leaned down, acted as though he'd picked up a rock and pretended to throw it into the river. The fact he had neither picked up a rock nor made a splash did not deter him from throwing several more imaginary rocks.

"Pretty tough to find a good skipping rock here," I offered.

He wound up and threw another, as though he intended for it to skip across the surface of the river. "Sure is. These pretend rocks don't skip more than three or four times before they sink."

I stood next to him and pretended to heave the biggest rock I was capable of lifting. For effect, I leapt back from the edge to avoid the splash it would have caused. It was strange. Although there was no rock and no splash, somehow there was. I didn't see it, but in the process of pretending I experienced it.

Apparently Finn had too. "That rock was huge! You almost soaked me!"

Mesmerized by the smiling face, in my mind I saw the little boy I remembered him to be. Squatting, clutching a handful of pebbles, the vision of him catapulted the handful into the water as he squealed with delight, which in memory was the crescendo of the symphony of rocks breaking the surface tension of the water.

"Why are you staring at me like that? It's kind of weird," he said.

I shook my head. "Sorry about that. I... you... "

"Did you have a movie of me playing in your head?"

"I did. How did you know?" I asked.

"How couldn't you? I'm totally awesome," he responded.

"Okay, now. Let's not get too much of an inflated head. I also remember that we couldn't get you to stop eating chalk," I asked.

"The palate of a two-year old is much like an out of tune piano," he said. "To get the right sound, you've got to go sharp and then flat to figure out what the real note is. How can you know what tastes good, if you've never figured out what tastes bad?"

"That makes sense but what does that have to do with you eating chalk all the time?"

"Well, it... I mean... I was only testing the flat side... you're it." No sooner had he finished saying it than he was on the other side of the field. I knew what he wanted to do and I was caught off guard by how much I wanted to as well. He wanted to play. So that's what we did.

We played a game of hyper speed tag, the goal being to touch the other person and then avoid him so he would remain "it". Next we went to the park. The slide that was uninteresting before came to life with Finn. Somehow his excitement made it exciting for me. We played hopscotch, we ran races (both with and without using our minds), I gave him piggyback rides and then he returned the favor. We sat underwater and counted the branches as they went by (there weren't enough fish).

"Best day ever," said Finn in our underwater playground.

As much as I wanted to agree, as the sun crept towards the western edge of the sky, a desire to return to Fiona and to Becky's dream grew until it had sucked the pleasure out of every thought and enjoyment and had left me in a state of desperate anticipation. "It was a fun day but I've got to get going. Maybe we can do this again tomorrow?"

"What's wrong, big brother?" asked Finn. "You seemed like you were having so much fun. Was it because I dominated you in all the races?"

"No. I just... I have something I need to go do tonight but I really want to spend more time with you. Why don't we do this again tomorrow?"

"Can I come with you?" he asked. "I may be your younger brother, but when it comes to this place, I'm pretty much the smartest guy you'll find around here."

It was getting dark and so was my mood. I was surprised at how impatient I felt. "No, you can't. I'm going to spend time with my friends tonight and I don't think it's a good idea if you come."

"I think you'll need help. Can I please come?"

Internal storm clouds hung over my consciousness, thunder and lightening threatened. If I was being honest with myself I would have admitted I didn't want him to come because somehow, somewhere I didn't feel right about what I was going to do. But I pushed that away because the rules were different here. I was going to make the most of this miserable existence. "What makes you think I need help?"

"The people you are now spending your time with…" he said.

"Were you spying on me? What's wrong with the people I spend time with?" I asked.

"Not spying. Just watching. I couldn't come see you right away, so I was waiting for the right time to come see you," he said.

"What do you mean you couldn't come see me right away? When did you first find me?"

"When you first came to the field," he said, eyes fixed on his feet.

"What? You saw everything that happened to me. You saw me struggling to figure this… place out and you just stood there?"

"I didn't see everything that happened. I was here at the reunion, but the timing wasn't right. I really wanted to help you. It was so hard for me not to help you. But I couldn't."

"What do you mean, you couldn't?"

"I can't say," he whispered. "The timing wasn't right. I was told the timing wasn't right."

"Who told you not to help?"

"I can't say." He reached for my arm. The instant he made contact, I saw the face of Chief, the same one who hated me. "It's for your own good and for the good of the family. If I tell you, it will ruin everything."

I pulled away from his touch and the image faded from my mind. "You just confirmed something for me."

Pain etched in his face, he asked, "What's that?"

"You really do have to look out for yourself first in this world. Everybody's already doing it, only some are more open than others. I don't know for sure who it is who's telling you what to do, but you should know whoever it is does not have what's best for you as the goal. You are being used. And what's worse, being used to use me. Do you even know why?"

"You don't understand, I do…"

"No, I do understand. Chief hates me. It makes perfect sense. And you're helping him." Finn reached for me again but I stepped away. "I've figured enough out to know who I should trust and who I shouldn't."

"Taven, slow down. Wait. It's not how it seems. Please, trust me."

I knew he was sincere, but I was also pretty sure he was deluded. "I will always love you, little brother, but if you're taking orders from someone like him and you can't tell me what they are... I have nothing more to say."

Before I could recoil, he grabbed my arm. A warmth filled me. I felt his sincerity although I was given no further visions in my mind. "Please don't be mad at me."

I hugged him. "I'll come find you again sometime and I hope you will have thought through what I had to say. The rules are different here. Everyone's got selfish motives. You've got to make sure they're in your best interest."

"What you're saying might seem like it makes sense to you, but it doesn't feel right to me, Taven. Does it feel right to you?"

I stepped back from him. "Doesn't feel right? I'll tell you what doesn't feel right to me. Being abandoned by a bunch of people that used to be my family. Having the only person who seemed like she was willing to help 'move on', whatever that means. Having a crazy uncle..."

"You don't know what you're talking about. Just be patient. It's only a matter of time before this will all make sense."

"I'm not sure what to tell you, Finn. I really feel like whatever family was in the other world... it isn't that here."

"You don't want to be my family?"

"I want to be your friend. I choose that but for now I've got to go. If I wait any longer I'm going to be late. I've got a dream to get to," I said.

"What do you mean dream, Taven? You haven't been in a dream, have you?" he asked.

His concern bounced off the hard crust of my excitement "Time to go."

The image of his outstretched hand, and his cry of "No" stuck in my mind as I pictured Becky's room.

Not what I expect in the dugout

Legs dangling over the side of the bed, my racing mind burning over the anticipated condemnation, I suffered as only the doomed can. The fifth Grade was going smoothly until a particularly brutal spelling test. I was sure I'd be grounded for a week. It's not that my parents were strict, but I couldn't see how I could be forgiven for getting a four out of ten.

My torment was interrupted by Finn, who dawdled into my room. "Tay... cawr?" he asked, a small toy car clutched in his pudgy hand.

"No Finn. I don't wanna play with you," I said, giving him a little push away from me.

Undaunted, he approached me again, and began driving his car on my knee. "Ha come?"

"Because I got a really big problem and I don't have time to play with you."

"Oh," he said, still using my leg as an off ramp, "Cawr?"

"No," I said taking the car from him. "I'm gonna tell Mom if you keep bugging' me." I remember expecting him to completely freak out in response to my taking his car. To my surprise, he simply stood and looked deeply into my eyes.

"Tay sad?" he asked. Without waiting for a reply he wrapped his little arms around my waist and squeezed. "Lub you, Tay."

I couldn't be mad at him, in fact, I didn't even feel so worried about my test anymore. I opened my eyes.

I sat on the floor in the middle of Becky's empty bedroom. I was the first to arrive. The teddy bear at the foot of the bed, the porcelain doll perched on the top of her shelf, the crayon-drawn picture of Becky's family, the hand-made quilt, each yarn carefully tied, spoke to me of the innocence of the little girl whose room I was in.

"You look like someone stole your puppy," said Fiona as she materialized in the room. Seeing her pierced the cloud that hung over me, but didn't disperse it. "Is everything alright?"

I stood and rubbed at the wrinkles in my pants, despite having no effect on them. I wondered whether a hug from her would help but no sooner had I though it than Ben and Dan arrived. They were intruders, intruders I was convinced would steal this opportunity from me if I squandered my time with Fiona again. "I was... I was thinking about my brother."

"Is something wrong?" she asked, grabbing my arm. Finn's touch was warm, hers was electric. "If there's anything I can do to help you, Taven..."

"Why are you being so nice to me? I just don't get it. You said the rules are different here. Why are you wasting time with me?" I asked.

"Are you worried about your brother?" she asked. "Were you looking for him? We can help you find him."

"But I already...I mean there's no point... he's already dead," I said. I don't know why I didn't tell her about me finding Finn. I guess I wasn't ready to open up any more quite yet.

"Taven, I don't know what you're feeling or why you're feeling it, but let me tell you something. Even if you find him, he's not going to say anything different than the rest of your family," she said in a breathy whisper. I opened my mouth, but quickly closed it deciding that I'd hear her out before divulging anything else. "He'll tell you that you should listen to your family, that you've got to fulfill a purpose that suits the family and that finding happiness isn't your purpose."

"How do you know that's what he'll say?"

"Because if he's anything like you, he'll care too much and he'll be susceptible to those who use family as an excuse to control everyone else." Fiona grabbed my arm again. The electricity of her touch was now so intense it was almost painful. Images of me being scolded by my parents, memories of my brief meeting with relatives here, flashed in my mind.

"I can tell what I'm saying hurts you. I don't want to hurt you." A vivid memory of the pain I experienced when I broke my leg on the playground in Grade Two briefly tormented me.

"I'm telling you because I don't want you to be hurt and to be caught up in what your family will try to do to you. Families hold you down." I now remembered almost, or at least feeling like I almost, drowned when I was eight. I couldn't remember being saved only the smothering of my lungs, my own inability to help myself despite desperate need. But I knew I'd been helped and strained for remembrance. As if in a glimmer I saw my dad's face and his hand. Then it was gone along with the brief feeling of relief.

"They set up boundaries to keep you bound to them, under their control." I was for an instant, the dog I saw muzzled and collared as a little boy, subject to pain if I disobeyed.

"They keep you from being happy because they're happier when you are under the delusional framework they've set up. I'm sure your brother is a great guy but he's a part of the system, a part of the framework. All he is going to do is try to get you back in line." Everything faded from view. It was as though I was transported somewhere else. The pain and the harsh memory, Fiona, Ben and Dan, were gone and Finn, as a little two-year-old boy, stood hand in hand with a little blond girl. The little girl hugged Finn and ran toward me with a paper in her hand. She handed it to me, then reached for me to hug her. I hugged her, then she ran back to Finn. I looked to the paper that contained four sentences. All else faded from my mind, I read. "Don't believe what I'm telling you. You can't let on that you know. Keep me safe. This is the only way."

The paper faded from memory although the writing lingered in my memory as Fiona, her face unchanged, came back into view and the electricity in my arm intensified. "Do you trust me?"

After what I had experienced, I had no idea what to think, let alone who to trust. "Can I trust you?"

Fiona placed her hands on my hips. "Yes." She drew herself slowly closer to me. "So are you going to let yourself be held back, or are you going to come and have some happiness with me?"

Flashes of the feeling of the touch of her hand, the warmth of her skin, her smell, overwhelmed my resolve and my desire overcame any and all hesitation. "I want to be happy."

Fiona was now within a hair of my lips. "Good."

"You're a lucky man to be getting some of that," said Ben. "You aren't going to play hero again and mess it up, are you?"

I'd forgotten Ben was even in the room but somehow, even though I was now aware, I was held by Fiona's eyes. "I definitely won't mess it up. Don't you have to make yourself scarce or something?"

"We've got to know you're not going to pull another stunt like you did last time," said Dan, whose words floated in the background, audible, but not really comprehensible.

He was there too. But it didn't matter. At that moment I was caught in her spell and every desire seemed to be focused on her. "I won't."

"Don't mind these two." Fiona glanced toward them and they were gone. "They're jealous. The truth is this girl isn't the only special one. You are too. And we need your help."

"You need me?" I asked.

"We do," she said, directing me to sit, then sitting next to me on the bed. "The gift that Becky has, her creativity and openness in dreams, well, it only lasts so long. She isn't the first and she won't be the last. Until we met you there were no more dreams that we could get into."

"There are millions of people. Why didn't you find somebody else?"

"You can't get into anybody's dreams. You can only get into the dreams of someone you've got a connection with," she said.

"You ran out of dreams?"

"It's not so much that we ran out of dreams, but the creativity only lasts for so long, and once that time period is over, there's no point going into someone's dreams. The trick is you can't go into someone's dreams if you don't have a connection with them," Fiona explained. "Becky, needs to be... willing... to have us into her dreams. When it comes to people with this special gift, the only way they'll be willing is if you have a connection. It's important to create new connections."

"New connections?" I asked.

"The best way to explain it is it's like a cell phone. You can only send text messages to people whose phone number you have. Dreams are like that. You've got to be familiar to the person to be able to communicate that way," she said.

"If you needed my connections that means I'm connected to Becky. How's that possible? I don't even know who she is."

"The best way to ruin a good time is with too many questions. Here she comes," said Fiona.

Becky entered the room, dressed in the same nightgown as last time. She knelt by her bed, mumbled some inaudible words, climbed into bed and slipped under the covers. She held them tightly across her chest. She closed her eyes. Her breath deepened, her face relaxed and she was asleep.

"This time you're going to get us in, Taven," said Fiona.

"I don't how to do that," I said.

"I'll teach you," she said. "First we don't want to end up in any dream. A part of what makes Becky special is that she lets you chose the place for the dream. You've got to have your mind on a place where we can be in control of the situation."

"Why do we need to be in control of the situation?" I asked.

"We're not going to have that much fun if we're in the middle of a war zone. There's no telling what the mind will do on its own," she said.

"I don't know. I guess we could use the mansion again," I suggested.

"I think that's a great idea. We also need a diversion," she said.

"Why do we need a diversion?" I asked.

"To keep Becky out of our way. I don't think we want her walking in on us," she said. Leaning in, she whispered, "and if Ben and Dan take care of the diversion, that keeps them out of the way too."

I gulped. "Okay."

"Once you've got the place for the dream in mind, put your hands on either side of her forehead. Once our hands are on your shoulders, like we did last time, place your head against hers and focus on entering her dreams. Don't stop no matter what happens," she said. "Ben. Dan. We're ready."

I stood feeling like I was caught in a current I was not strong enough to paddle against. "Okay."

"Are you ready?" she asked.

"Yes," I lied.

"Then do it and get ready for the time of your life."

I hesitantly put my hands on either side of Becky's head. The moment I did, it was as though I could hear her voice pleading with me to leave her alone, not to torment her.

"No matter what," said Fiona, as though she knew exactly what was happening. "Remember, she has a special gift. Remember that it's only a dream."

I ignored Becky's pleas, dismissing them as my own imagination. I held my head to hers and focused on entering her dream. Her cries were cut short and all that remained was blackness.

"Concentrate on the mansion," a bodiless voice echoed.

I scrambled in memory for a mental image of the mansion, but despite remembering being there, I was unable to conjure a complete picture of the place.

"Concentrate. Draw it in your mind," the voice encouraged.

I pulled out my mental crayons, and attempted to draw the line of trees, but the crayons refused to release their respective colors to my mental canvass. I tried to use mental paints, mental pastels, mental pens, but to no avail. I could not bring myself to draw that mansion. And at that moment I realized I really didn't want to. Whether or not Becky was affected by the dream, I didn't want to go back to the place where she had been tormented.

I relaxed and the drawing implements that had refused to obey my commands now took on a life of their own and outlined a baseball field. Before I knew it I was standing a baseball toss away from a ball diamond, with a covered dugout between third base and home, next to my old hot dog cart. The rubber grip on the handle I used to push it was more pleasant to the touch than I ever remembered it being.

"This is not the mansion," the same bodiless voice said, "But this will do."

Now that my hot dog cart was out of my mind and tangibly beside me, it was surprisingly satisfying. And it was fully stocked. I couldn't help but turn on the grill, slice open a package of hot dogs and throw two of them on the grill. Maybe it wouldn't be the most romantic meal, but it was a meal, and I'd be able to taste it. I could feel myself salivating. It took all my resolve not to drink the ketchup.

"What do you want me to look like?" the voice asked, as I greedily assembled the first hot dog and shoved it into my mouth. The combination of the relish and ketchup over the processed meat and not freshly baked bun was heavenly. "Do you care more about that hot dog than me?"

I was tempted to say yes. If the rules were different here, why couldn't I care more about what I wanted at that very moment more than anything else? But I decided that wasn't how I wanted to be. "No. But I made one for you too."

"I'm sure it tastes great, Taven, but you're the only treat I'm interested in right now. What do you want me to look like," she said. "I can be anything you want."

I gulped and it wasn't because of the hot dog. I'd never thought of a human relationship as being a pick a part type of

TAVEN'S DEPARTING

arrangement. But maybe the hot dogs were a sign. You can put together the hot dog you want, with the condiments you want. Maybe that's how relationships work here. It's better because you can get what you want. As compelling as these ideas were to me, my stomach turned as though the hot dog I ate had gone bad in every possible way. But I was here, and if no one was going to get hurt, why not go ahead?

I mentally constructed the portrayal of beauty that I saw on so many supermarket magazine stands, a smiling woman whose face had been airbrushed and bodily dimensions had been digitally altered, a beauty that is satisfied in being little more than a sugary treat for the eyes.

But that wasn't how I wanted to be and because it wasn't how I wanted to be, it wasn't what I wanted. I wanted something real, something reciprocal, something substantial. And I wanted to be accepted for who I was. Again I cleared my mind and one face came to me, and only one face. It belonged to Eve.

Instantly she stood next to me. The last bit of my hot dog dangling in my hand, I scrambled to offer her the other. She reached out with her hand, slightly smaller than mine, skin so smooth, her wrist covered by the sleeve of her sweater. As our hands touched, I was thrown back into a stream memories. Time and time again she had come to my cart. She laughed with me. She talked with me. Time and time again, I handed her whatever it was

163

she had ordered, purposely placing my hand in a way that she would have to touch it when she took what she had purchased, every contact sending a thrill through my body.

Here she was in her straight cut jeans with flip-flop sandals on her feet. There was no mixing and matching of parts, no attempt to create magazine type of appeal, but to me, this was what beauty was.

"This is what you wanted?" asked Fiona, not veiling her surprise.

It was. It didn't matter that I couldn't remember anything about her after the horrifying police encounter. It didn't matter that it was probably because she had shunned me. I didn't remember her ever trying to allure me with her looks, but she always was kind and gentle. She always made me feel special. Her visits to my vending cart always made my day. "I guess so," I responded.

"You guess so," she said. "If this is what you want, don't you want me to be dressed differently... or rather less dressed."

I looked into those eyes and could not imagine doing anything to the person they belonged to, even in a dream, that would in any way desecrate her. "No. It's not that. I don't know what's happening. I know the girl you look like but..."

"I can be anyone you want. Anyone," she said. "Things are different here. How many times do I have to tell you? And now you are on the verge of losing me. Losing my help, losing this opportunity, and losing my friendship. You are dead. Relationships don't matter anymore. What matters is one thing, and that is you."

"What about you? Don't you matter? Doesn't it bother you that you have to look like someone other than yourself?" I asked.

"It doesn't matter what I was. I don't remember what I looked like and it doesn't matter. Here I am. Here I exist. That is what defines me. Appearances change. Friends change. Families change. But what remains constant is existence and my efforts to exist the way I want to. And I want to be happy," she said.

"Does this really make you happy?" I asked. "Pretending to be someone else?"

"Just stop thinking about her and enjoy this time with me. You won't regret it," she said.

"That's the problem. When I look at you I can't stop thinking about her and I'm starting to realize that I do regret it."

"No. The problem is you won't forget her. And what is there to regret? You are not alive. The same rules do not apply. Forget about what doesn't matter anymore. All that is keeping you from happiness is your own inability to let go of what doesn't matter anymore," she said.

"You're right. I won't let go but it's not because it doesn't matter. It does. I've already come too far down a path that I never should have followed. Finn was right."

"Finn's your brother, isn't he?" Fiona asked, changing from Eve, to the appearance she had in the mortal world.

"Yes."

"Didn't I warn you about what he'd try to do? How he'd try to catch you in the family net?" she asked.

"What you're saying makes sense, but it doesn't feel right."

"That's because you've been trained all your ..."

"Give me back my hot dog," I said. "Whatever we had, we're through. Thank you for helping me, but I can't do this anymore."

She dropped the hot dog on the ground and stomped on it. "You're thanks are worth about as much as this disgusting hot dog." She was gone. I popped that last bit of my hot dog into my mouth. It had gone bitter, matching the contents of my stomach. I spat the remnants on the ground.

An ear-piercing scream tore me from reflecting on everything that had just happened.

I ran away from my cart and toward the shelter along the third baseline where I thought the scream had come from. When I arrived, I found the shelter was hollowed out and at the bottom of a flight of stairs was an open door. Sensing I would find Becky if I descended the stairs, I went. Through the door was a tiny room, but it was not the size of the room that first caught my attention, but the occupants. In this room, the walls, floor and roof made entirely of earth, smelling of dank undergrowth, were three rotting corpses, pawing at Becky, their decomposed hands profaning the innocence of this girl. I grabbed the leg of the one closest to me and drug it out of the room. Stepping on its back, I went for the second, but was thrown off balance when the first stood.

"Back off, Taven," a familiar voice grumbled from the first being as it stood then kicked me, sending me halfway up the stairs. Unable to stand, I rolled myself down the stairs and drug myself back to the room. Before I could get to them the door shut and a whisper sounded throughout the dream "You're worthless" and hung in the air like a poisonous gas.

"Becky, are you alright?" I stood and reached for the door and tore it open. "Leave her alone." I charged the group. "She's a little girl."

The room was now immense and the wraiths were on the other side of it.

Becky screamed again.

I was back in her bedroom, standing over this little girl. She had an absolute look of torment on her face.

"Nice one, loser," Dan called from behind me. "You really saved her this time. How did you like your flight up the stairs?"

"Trying to be the hero again?" Ben added. "The one thing you've got in common with a hero is that you're as delusional, but that's about it.

Fiona strode up to me and stroked her finger across my face. There was no more seduction in her comportment, only cold solemnity. "Thanks for the way in, Taven. We couldn't have gotten into her dreams except with your help."

"I'm not letting you in again," I said.

"Who said you need to let us in again?" she said.

"Then why did you bring me in again? Why did you…"

Fiona's face was emotionless. "I've decided it is no longer in my best interest to be with you. You are clearly uninterested. But she is in my best interest. Frequenting her dreams has been, and will be, most rewarding."

"What kind of devil torments a little girl for her own pleasure?"

"Who said anything about pleasure?" Fiona asked in response.

"I won't let you hurt her again."

Ben and Dan laughed. Fiona revealed no emotion. "Oh, Taven. How will you do that?"

She was right. Everything I knew, or most of what I knew, I'd learned from them. How was I going to stop them? "So what? What's the worst you're going to do? Cause a few nightmares? She'll forget about you in the morning."

"All we can do is cause nightmares? If only that were the case. Until next time, " said Fiona, as she, Ben and Dan vanished.

Things get worse

Becky sat up, looking as though she had not slept in days, far too much care etched on her ten year-old face. Her eyes, distant and vacant, fixed on the teddy bear at the foot of her bed. Tears streaked down her cheeks. I had waited for her to wake up. I wanted some assurance I'd not harmed her. "She's going to be okay. It was only a dream. She'll get over it."

"Becky, it's time to get up. You've got school today." It was an unfamiliar woman's voice from outside the room.

"What's the point," Becky mumbled, slowly getting out of bed.

"You're going to be okay," I said. But she didn't hear me or at least, didn't let on if she had. I needed to know she was going to be okay so I followed her as she left her room and descended the stairs. I stopped short of the kitchen table and stood in the living room that adjoined the space, which was nothing like the one from my memories, the one I thought was mine. The carpet was long and looked soft, but I felt nothing other than a flowing and ebbing concern that I'd done more harm to this innocent girl than I had realized.

Becky hardly looked up as she passed the woman from the hallway portraits. She slumped in her chair at the kitchen table. Her mother walked behind her and placed her hands on the back of Becky's chair. "You look so sad. What's wrong, sweetheart?"

"Me," Becky said.

"What are you talking about?" The woman took the chair next to Becky. When Becky looked away, she slid Becky's chair so it faced her.

"I'm... I'm..." Becky looked up and sobbed, "I'm worthless."

The woman drew Becky towards her, but I could see that Becky was rigid. "You are an amazing little girl. You're smart, you're talented..."

"You have to say that. You're my mom. I'm a loser. I know it."

"No, I do not have to say that. Did something happen at school?"

"No," Becky responded. My fear built and arched over me, I was unable to move, I was about to be crushed by it.

"Did your dad or I do something to you?"

"I don't know what it is. I just know I'm worthless." A tsunami of guilt rode over me. I knew why she felt that way. I was there. I was the reason they got in.

I needed help to help her and my only hope was back at my park. I walked over to Becky and put my hand on her shoulder. "I will help you. Don't give up." It seemed like she melted into her mother at my touch, but I knew I was only imagining things. I drew the field in my mind.

"Finn. Finn! I need your help. Please help me. Please forgive me!" I expected he would be standing there waiting for me, but he wasn't. I focused and was in the mortal world. The moon was out and stars shone down on me. The majesty of the heavens was a fitting compliment to how small I was feeling at that moment. "Finn!"

He was nowhere to be seen. I unfocused my eyes and returned to the hazy nether world. "Finn? Auntie Sophie? Uncle Bennett? I'm here. I need your help. Please help me."

I sat down, determined to find a way to find them. If they didn't come to me, I'd go to them. I braced myself for the attempt, not yet sure what the attempt was going to be, when the same squirrel I'd seen before scurried across a branch from the tree that hung over my head. He watched me, looking as interested in what I would have to say as a squirrel possibly could. "Is there any way back from where I am? I've really messed up. Can you help me find my brother? If you can, please help me."

The squirrel leapt from the branch to my lap. It's almost as though he understood me. More than understood, he empathized with me. I reached out and with a single finger stroked the darker band of fur along his side. As always, there was no physical sensation accompanying my touching; however, the squirrel responded as though he had felt everything. I tried it again, and again the squirrel responded as though I'd given him a sublime scratching. Finding this to be a salve to my wounded conscience, I continued to oblige him.

"Do you think if you scratch her long enough she'll start speaking English?"

I turned around and there was my brother, no longer in his vibrant green and embarrassing tights, but now in a dark blue business suit with a hardly noticeable pin stripe, shiny black dress shoes, an unexceptional white shirt and an unassuming grey tie. This dull look, which seemed to be having its effect on Finn's personality, ignited the guilt I'd assuaged by petting the squirrel. "Finn." I carefully took the squirrel in my hands and stood to face my brother. "I really messed up. I should have listened to what you had to say. I've ruined everything..."

"Hold that thought," said Finn, as he proceeded to squeak and exhale. The squirrel became animated and squeaked and exhaled in response. Finn laughed. The squirrel squeaked in my direction, Finn nodded and the squirrel jumped from my hands and bounded to a tree not far from us. "Squirrel is surprisingly easy to pick up. Instead of trying to understand the sounds that come into your ears and speak the words that come from your brain, just feel the conversation. It's actually a far more accurate way to understand what is really intended," he said, still somber as his suit.

"So what did he say?" I asked. "Did he tell you all the terrible things I've done."

"He who?" Finn responded.

"He... the squirrel," I said.

"I don't know what you're talking about," Finn said, the right half of his lip creaking upwards.

"The squirrel that was right here in my hand," I said, pointing as though Finn needed directions to figure it out. "The one you were talking to."

"Oh, that squirrel," he said, exaggerating his response. "He is a she. What made you think she is a he?"

I looked over to the squirrel, perched in the tree, black eyes fixed on us, seeming as though she was very interested in our conversation. "I don't know. I guess I always thought of squirrels as being boys... can she understand what we're saying?"

"Yep."

"But I knew right away she was different..."

"Taven."

"What?"

"You're not helping things."

"Can you tell her sorry for calling her a him?"

"I already did."

"Thanks. Finn, I need your help."

Finn motioned for me to come closer. Guarding his lips from the view of the squirrel with his hand he said, "Stop worrying about her so much. Like I told you, I already told her you were sorry. She's very forgiving. Besides, I think she likes you."

"What I meant was..." I was about to ask about Becky, about the dreams, but as much as I wanted to help her, I didn't think a few carefree moments with my brother change things. "So, what you're saying is all I have to do to be able to communicate with squirrels is to make sounds that match what I am feeling?"

"With your rage you'll scare the squirrel away. I think you need to calm down first. Breathe with me."

"Maybe later, how could she feel me scratching her?" I asked.

"Yep, you must really hit a sweet spot. Her leg was kicking and everything," said Finn, mimicking the squirrels actions.

"Was it in a dream? I mean did I let it in my dreams so it could feel me touching it?"

"I'm not sure I understand what you're talking about, but it had nothing to do with dreams," he said.

"How could she feel my touch?"

"Because you meant it when you did it. We don't *feel* the same way here. We can't physically touch here because we don't have a physical body. That doesn't mean we can't learn to experience the world around us other than by the five senses. All you've got to do is be open to new ways of experiencing, which are different to the way things are experienced by a physical body."

"Okay? So how do I do it?"

"It's actually a lot like my being able to speak squirrel. I focus on what I'm feeling and what the squirrel is feeling and then my mode of communication carries the understanding. If instead of waiting for the physical touch, you concentrate on your own feelings for that person and open yourself to the feelings that person is communicating by that touch, you can, in a manner of speaking, feel their touch. Let me show you. Big brother, gimme a hug."

I opened my arms and my brother, unhesitatingly embraced me fully. I didn't feel anything at first, no press of his arms, but willing to believe his words, I concentrated on what I felt and the feelings he was trying to convey with his hug. It was hard to concentrate, images of my failings, thoughts of the harm I'd done to Becky intruded; however, in spite of these interruptions, I felt a ring of warmth where his arms were.

"I love you, big brother," said Finn. "I think you are the best."

Tingles sparkled up and down my spine, up to the top of my head and down to the tips of my toes, like tens of thousands of fans cheering for me, believing in me, amazed by all that I was doing and wanting to see what I would do next. For that moment, I felt like I was everything he thought me to be.

"Now," he continued, "let's try the hug again. You seemed like you were having a hard time concentrating. Are you ready? Are you focused?"

I closed my eyes and focused on my feelings about my brother and the feelings he was demonstrating to me by his action. The same rush of excitement as when he told me he loved me returned. No self-accusing memories this time as I experienced the thrill of the expression more intensely around my back where his arms were wrapped. "Do you feel it big brother?"

"I do." The glow of the experience slowly faded, and I relished in its warmth. I half expected that when it left completely, I would feel like I needed another hug to make me feel better, but the reality was one hug had lifted me so that I didn't feel so needy. It gave me cause to believe in myself.

"Now you know how the squirrel could feel what you were doing." Finn's face became very serious. "So, why did you ask whether the squirrel was feeling in your dreams?"

Finn's question crashed through the protective veneer of the hug and dropped me into the icy cold reality of the regrettable decisions I had made. I was, however, sufficiently embarrassed by my actions that I didn't really want to immediately reveal the full extent of my poor choices to my two-year old brother. "Why do you ask?"

"Because being in someone else's dream is very dangerous," he said.

"Why?" I asked.

He looked at me as though I should already know, but continued, "Because it does serious harm to the person who enters the dream and to the person having the dream."

"Harm?" I asked now feeling like I was about to get some really bad news from a doctor.

"Yes, harm. People who continually enter into dreams lose all sense of self. They forget who they are because they have no purpose other than pleasure. Continued experiences are required to overcome the emptiness of having no purpose outside of the dream. They're emptied out, only to be filled by whatever can offer them what they want."

I knew what Finn was talking about. I remembered the craving but I was able to control it, wasn't I? I chose to be good, I chose to be more than what I wanted. "How is it that going into someone's dreams harms another person?"

"Would you want someone else in your thoughts with an ability to permanently influence them? No matter how good their intentions were? The dreamer has no choice about whether or not the person will enter the dream, and whether the dream is a nice one or not. The absence of choice destroys identity over time. Suggestions made in a dream stick. Take Janice," Finn said, grabbing my hand.

In an instant we were in what looked like the dressing room of a movie star. Slumped in a chair in front of the mirror, buried under layers of heavy make-up, sat a woman, dressed as though she were ready to go on stage. She looked like the world says a beautiful woman should look. Her body was thin in *acceptable* places, and more voluptuous in the *right* places, her long hair adorned her shoulders, her lips were full, her nose was thin and her eyelashes hung like awnings. Alluringly empty, her large eyes suggested the hurt inside.

"This is Janice," said Finn. "Her father, who died when she was a small girl, well meaning, figured out by chance how to enter her dream. While there, he told her she was the most beautiful girl in the world, a fair thing for a father to say. The problem was in that setting she believed it literally. And she held to it. To the father's great chagrin, she has lived out her life with vanity as her driving principle. Although opportunity has come to her because of her confidence and beauty, she's lost everything else in the process."

"What do you mean by everything else?"

"The important stuff."

"What's the important stuff?"

"Don't you know, big brother?"

"Is there no hope for Janice? I mean, can't she choose to change?"

"I don't know. The point is dreams are dangerous even when a person has the best of intentions. The father mourns for his daughter but he craves a repeat of the experience of the dream. Can you imagine what it would be like to want what you don't want: to cause further harm to your daughter because it feels good to you? What's worse is that he has no idea how to help Janice and can't help her because he won't be entering her dreams ever again." Finn grabbed my hand again and we were back in the hazy clearing.

"The father can't go back into her dreams?"

"That's what Chief said."

"How does he know?"

"I don't know," said Finn. "He just does."

Knowing I was going to reveal my guilt by asking the question, but needing to know what he thought, I asked, "Do you think there any hope for people who go in dreams? For the people whose dreams they go into?"

"I don't know," he said. "But I haven't heard of it ever working out."

Could it be that I was lost? I reviewed everything that had happened and I mourned. There was no doubt I had made bad decisions, but there was nothing, at least in my view, that would justly condemn me as a lost soul. Especially since I now felt no desire to go into a dream other than to help Becky. I trusted Finn but deep down I knew there had to be a way. I would do anything to find it. I wasn't a parasite. I wouldn't be a parasite. He wasn't describing me. And I would do whatever it took to help Becky. "Can't you fix someone without hope?"

"I don't know."

He knew I had already been in a dream, but the idea of admitting I had been in dreams again was like swallowing barbed wire. As terrible as I knew it would be, I knew what I had to do. "I've been in two dreams but I didn't want to hurt anybody."

"Oh."

"But it's worse. The people I brought into the girl's dream... they were... they are trying to destroy her."

"You brought someone else into the dreams," Finn looked to the ground and then to me. "Who are they?"

I didn't know much of anything beyond their names. I felt extremely foolish. "Fiona, Ben and Dan."

"Are they family members?" he asked.

"How would I know that? I know they don't like family and Fiona told me she needed me to get into the dream," I said.

"Not good... We'll work through this together. We can fix this together," he said, pacing in front of me.

"How do you know we can fix it? You just said you didn't know if fixing it is possible," I said, unnerved by his pacing.

"I don't know how but there's got to be a way. This isn't what we planned," he said.

"What did you plan?" I asked.

"I wouldn't worry about that. Taven, those people you brought in the dream... you gave them the family connection. They don't need you to enter any dream of any living person connected to you," he said.

"Any one?" My thoughts were on Eve. "Are you saying I've doomed our family?"

"No I'm saying we should focus on the real problem," he said. "What's the name of the girl?"

"Her name is Becky. I didn't even know I was connected to her," I replied.

"Her name doesn't ring a bell, but Chief will know. We need to figure out a plan to guard her, to help her if we can," he said.

"What about everyone else? How do you know they're going after her? Couldn't they go after anyone I'm connected with?" I asked.

"They could. But their usual pattern is to follow the path of least resistance. Some people are resistant to them. It's highly unlikely they would work on someone other than Becky when they know she's not going to be able to resist their efforts to enter her dreams," he said.

"I need to go back into her dreams," I said.

"What?" asked Finn. "Didn't you hear anything I told you? About Janice? You've got to let it go or…"

"The first time I was with them, Becky was in a room all by herself and was assaulted by monsters. I tried to fight them off but when I was about to be smashed, she screamed and I wasn't in the dream anymore. The next time I was there, she was alone in a dugout and was then surrounded by living skeletons, which whispered over and over that she had no hope. They stole her hope by defeating her in her dream. If we go in and rescue her, we might be able to give her hope."

"Do you remember what I told you about Janice? Her father was trying to help her."

"Yes, but I... I mean we can do it together. I'm not effected by the dreams the way you describe. I mean I was, but not anymore. I was able to choose to change, to let it go. And Becky, I saw her, she's already going down. We've got to try something and if this is all we've got, I need to try."

"You remember that I told you this hasn't worked out before?"

I did but somehow I knew it was different this time because I was different. "I do. But do you trust your big brother?"

"You mean your plan is for us to go into Becky's dreams and fight off the bad guys," Finn beamed, but the smile faded quickly. "Sounds like fun, but we can't do it."

"Why not?"

For the first time since I'd re-met him, Finn seemed genuinely agitated. "Didn't anyone tell you to stay out of dreams? It's one of the family laws. We stay out of dreams to keep safe, to keep each other safe."

"But I've already been. And because I went, Fiona, Ben and Dan have entered the family connection. If we don't try to stop them, based on what you told me our entire living family is doomed. That's why we have to try."

"I don't know," Finn said quietly.

"Then I'm going into her dreams. I'm going to fight off those monsters. I'm going to give her hope," I said, stepping away from Finn.

"Taven, I can't let you do that. Another family law is that we make sure that people stay out of dreams, and if they've been into them, to let the family know. It's against everything I know to let you go back into the dream. The family has to know. I'm sorry."

"What do you mean you're sorry?"

Finn closed his eyes and whispered, "I need you."

The day of reckoning

First to arrive was Uncle Bennett, who was almost immediately joined by other family members. I could hear him reporting on his little shepherd boy above the greetings of yet more relatives. At last, and more frightening than I had anticipated, Chief, still looking as old as ever, and great great grandma White, looking young and vibrant, an extraordinarily odd couple, arrived.

I was having a case of déjà vu I wasn't in any way prepared to have. Despite having a pretty good sense of how they would arrive, I hadn't prepared myself emotionally for the experience of having to face them, apologize and then tell them I'd doomed the whole family. Standing in their midst, I had never felt more alone and apart. "What's going to happen, Finn?"

"I don't know, Taven, but I'm not going to let anything bad happen to you," he whispered.

The fact my parents couldn't be there, or I assumed they couldn't, I didn't know whether living people could be a part of this type of gathering, was magnified by the fact that one of my principal advocates among the dead was missing: Auntie Sophie.

The concept of moving on had seemed like nothing more than a passing reference, but the stark reality now stood before me as impassable as a concrete blockade. She would not be there to help me.

"Alright everyone," said Chief, sounding as though his voice box were one hundred and eighty years old, "let us gather together for the council called by our young Finn.

I turned to Finn and whispered, "Council? All you said was I need you. Am I on trial?"

He whispered, using his hand to shield his mouth "All they know is I called for advice. They don't know anything else... I don't think."

And then it dawned on me, "That's why you're dressed in this suit. You're my lawyer..."

But before Finn could answer, he was interrupted by Chief, who stood alone in front of three groups of relatives seated in groups of twenty, each group divided into four rows of five. "Alright, Finn, why have you called this council? And while explaining, please speak clearly and loudly, for the benefit of us elderly folk. Also, we don't want any of the foolishness we had in the whole ground hog's shadow incident. This isn't another one of your jokes, is it?"

Standing at attention, Finn barked, "No, sir."

Chief moaned, then said, "Please let us know why you've called us."

"Do you remember the time when you once told me there was something really important that I should always remember and not forget that would be very important for me to report if I learned of it?" asked Finn.

"What is he talking about?" Chief asked me.

I wondered to myself why it was that Finn, now in the roll of advocate, had again taken on his sillier alter ego. "What he means is…"

"I called this meeting because… because… I missed everyone," Finn blurted.

"How many times do I need to remind you the council is for very important matters and not because you want to see us? That is why we have regular celebrations," Chief said. I wished I'd known about these parties before joining up with the worst of the worst. Patience was never one of my strongest virtues. He turned back to the three groups. "Alright everyone. False alarm. It was very nice to see…"

"Wait," Finn interrupted.

Clearly unimpressed, Chief turned back to Finn and asked, "What is it, Finn?"

"There might be some ppl n drms tvn ddn mn too," Finn mumbled.

"Are you going to continue making a mockery of..." shouted Chief until he was interrupted by his wife, who simply cleared her throat. "What I mean is can you please speak more clearly so I can understand why it is you called us here?"

As anxious as I was to get out of this situation unscathed, I knew Finn simply did not want to do anything that would get me in trouble. I said, "I went into..."

"Ignore Taven. Ignore him. He's crazy. Had a long day. The reason I called this council is because, umm, there's a problem with dreams and our family," said Finn.

Chief shuffled towards Finn and asked, "Do you mean what I think you mean?"

"I think so," said Finn, nodding.

"Whose dreams have been penetrated?" asked Chief.

"It's nothing to worry about at all," Finn said.

"Whose dreams?"

"Only one girl," Finn replied. "A girl named Becky."

Chief pulled at his chin, stubbled by short white hairs. "Hmm. There is no Becky in our connections. You must be mistaken."

"Yep, I must be."

"But," said Chief, bringing Finn back to attention, "You wouldn't have brought this up unless..." Chief looked right at me, "unless she was part of the family."

"She might be," Finn said.

"How exactly is it that you found out about this Becky, Finn?" asked Chief. Finn might as well have been under the bright light, in the uncomfortable chair, at the empty table, confined in the stuffy interrogation room, matched beyond his wits.

"A little birdie told me?" said Finn.

"Were you in a dream? Did you go into this Becky's dream?" asked Chief. The gasps of the groups of twenty were audible.

Finn did not move a muscle.

"Answer the question."

"I know her name is Becky because…" I began. The impact of all eyes turning to me was tangible. "because I was with…"

"No, Taven. I was… I was in the dream. That's how I knew," said Finn, his hand over my mouth. Strangely, I was unable to speak while he held his hand over it.

With all the strength I could muster, I pulled his arm and said, "I was with them in her dream. Finn had nothing to do with it. He found me and tried to keep me out of trouble but the truth is I was in trouble before he found me and I wasn't smart enough to listen to him. Becky's in danger and it's my fault."

There was an another gasp from the crowd. Finn slouched, "No Taven."

"Them? You were in a dream?" Chief asked, his gaze burning into me.

I hoped if I explained what had happened, Chief might understand. I told them about my adventures downtown, about Fiona rescuing me, about how I went into the dream not really knowing it was wrong. How I tried to rescue Becky. How Fiona, Ben and Dan were trying to destroy her.

"You went into her dream? How could you? Your uncle Bennett warned you not to."

"I didn't understand…"

I was interrupted by Chief. "It doesn't matter if you didn't understand. The problem remains and now we have no choice."

"He didn't know he was doing harm," burst out Finn. "I know Taven. He wouldn't hurt a fly. Not on purpose any way. He can fix it. I know he can. He's different."

"You've done all you need to here Finn," said Chief.

"What do you mean?" asked Finn.

"You did your job. I commend you for being trustworthy in this most difficult situation," he said.

Finn stepped towards Chief. "I'm not going to let you hurt my brother. He's good. Just like you said. He'll open new..."

"That's enough Finn. You've got to learn when to stop. We've got to remove the connection... this 'Becky' will be carved out," said Chief to another round of gasps. "And so will you," Chief said pointing to me. "By carving this Becky out, we'll sever her connection with us, but also with these monsters, these dream junkies. It's a shame we can't do anything to repair the damage caused by one of our own, but I fear it is irreparable. This girl will always suffer as a result of their devilry and your foolishness. By carving you out, we spare our family and the innocent living from the same fate."

The buzz from the crowd of relatives grew, and Chief turned and motioned for them to calm down. Finn was trembling. I had never seen a more distraught face.

I put my arm around him and whispered into his ear, "Finn. Don't worry about it. I don't mind not knowing the combination to the family. It's better this way. It's clear I can't be trusted. Calm down. It'll be okay."

Finn turned to face me and said, "It's not okay. It's more than a combination, Taven! It's what connects us. It's what helps us to find each other. Without it, time will cause us to forget each other. You will be forgotten by me and you will forget yourself! Connection informs identity. You won't know me and I won't know you." He was hysterical. "You aren't what you think you are. A few mistakes doesn't make a bad person. Owning up to the mistakes and caring about those who are affected by them proves it. You will change our family."

"I'm not going to forget who I am," I said.

"Yes you will. And you will be alone every day losing more of yourself. Cut off from memory. Cut off from real companionship. I can't let you go through that. I meant it when I said I thought you were great."

"It's alright…" I began.

Before I could continue, Finn walked over to Chief, tapped him on the shoulder and shouted, "then you need to carve out both of us. At least Taven won't be alone then."

All three groups of twenty shouted a unanimous, "No". They were now on their feet, the precise words of the jumble of protestations was incomprehensible but the message was very understandable; the family was not onside with Finn being cut off. And how could they be.

In response, Finn, resolute, responded, "If you won't cut me off with my brother, then I'll do something to be cut off. He's not going to suffer alone. I'll... I will enter a dream and then you'll have to."

This was out of control. My innocent much beloved brother was about to join me in my punishment for no apparent reason other than he couldn't bear for me to be the only one to suffer it. This was more than I could take. I'd rather lose myself than be the cause of the loss of my brother. "Finn, you can't do this. I made the choice to make the wrong friends. I ignored Uncle Bennett's advice. I chose to go into the dream. I chose to ignore what you told me."

"But you didn't know. No one told you how serious what you were doing was," Finn said. "And you always tried to make it better. Just like Chief said you would."

"It doesn't change the fact that I did it and now I have to face the consequence of the harm I've caused."

"I'm not going to let you suffer alone. I may forget myself and you, but I will never leave you. If I've got to tie a string to your leg and to my leg, I will be with you," Finn said.

"Maybe neither of us need to be carved out." I turned away from my brother and shouted over the rumble of the crowd, "Before any one is removed from the family, will you hear me out?"

The effect was instant silence. Chief, looking older and more weatherworn than ever, spoke. "Of course. Mistakes... stupid mistakes aside, I don't want to carve you out and I certainly don't want to carve out your brother, no matter how annoying he can be. If there was any other way of stopping this, we would do it."

I'm not sure where it came from, whether it was from my brother's confidence in me, or hearing that Chief had said that I would make things better, or some other source or from myself, but I knew I could make things better. At that moment I didn't know how, but I was certain a way would present itself if I took a path back through the dreams. I'd never been as sure about anything. And so I spoke. "There is. But to do it, it'll take something from all the family. My heart tells me we'll all be better for it. I've always wanted to make a difference. To leave my mark on the world for the better. My path hasn't led me there, but I know it's not too late because I have an amazing brother who believes in me. I'm not affected by the dreams. I have no desire to go back in. At first I felt the yearnings to have the experience of a physical body but I didn't let it decide what I would do and now, well, now I only want to help Becky. That's why I can make a difference. Fiona, Dan and Ben have convinced a little girl that she's worthless. I don't believe the living are defenseless from those kind of lies. I don't know much about Becky, but I know she's not worthless. I believe we can help. Aren't there some dreams that can't be penetrated? Maybe we can help our family to resist, to expel or, even better, to control. It would tear me apart to know I was the reason Fiona was able to destroy this innocent little girl. Please give me a chance to try. I know I can do it. Please help me to do it. I took the wrong path to get here, to put an innocent girl at risk, to cause her suffering, but I believe good can come of it but I'll need you to forgive me, and to trust me. I need you to keep me in the family, for now at least."

"How do you know any of this is possible?" asked a much-softened Chief.

"I just do. Here." I pointed to my heart.

"How do you propose to bring hope? We cannot communicate with the living so easily, as I am sure you have discovered," said Chief.

197

"I don't know, but unless you can tell me it's not possible, I do think it's worth trying for my life's sake, for Becky's life sake and for the potential of strengthening the entire family," I said.

There was a long, tense silence, broken by Chief. "I can't tell you it's not possible," he paused again, "what you are proposing goes way beyond just our family, but how are you going to do it?"

Gathering my courage, I said, "By going back into her dreams…"

It was as though what I said flipped the energy switch in Chief. "Going into her dreams? Don't you realize this is the type of behavior we are trying to stop? The danger we are trying to stop? No. Our conversation ends here. I'm sorry boys, but this is the way it has to be."

"No, it doesn't have to be this way," I said. "I can't tell you how it's going to work out. But somehow I know you will not be making a mistake by giving me a chance. I was strong enough to fight for Becky then, and I have to believe I will be strong enough later. Besides, even if I did make it worse, you could cut me off then. At least give me a chance."

Chief groaned within himself. "I'm not sure it's that simple," Chief walked towards me, "and there's Janice."

I pulled away. "I know about Janice but I'm not sure her situation is everyone's situation. Janice chose where she is. Her father may have planted a seed, but she choose to water it and let it grow. I don't believe she was forced into anything."

"Even if you could give Becky hope, by keeping you connected those fiends could move on to someone else," Chief said.

"Then we would meet them wherever they went," responded Finn. "Imagine how much stronger our family would be having learned to face and defeat those monsters. You knew dreams were going to decide the fate of our family. I know you thought we were in danger of heading down the same path as other families but you told me that Taven had a power…"

"That's enough Finn," Chief warned.

"Not, it's not enough. You told me he could save the family and beyond. If that's true, then maybe, I mean, this is the way."

"I could have been wrong. Especially given the circumstance." Chief turned to me. "How do you know that you can defeat them? How do you intend to stop them?"

"By standing against them," I responded. I was going to say we could capture them and carve them out, but the image of the little girl flashed in my mind. We couldn't do that yet.

Chief spoke before I had a chance to figure out what to say next. "How can you be so sure you will be able to overpower them? Do you even know who they really are? This isn't the time or the place, but if you knew who you were up against, you would not be so bold to propose what you are proposing."

"You're right. I don't know how, but I do know what needs to be done. And I believe I can do it if you'll give me the chance," I said.

"We can beat them," said Finn.

"We can beat them," I repeated.

"You risk further harm to Becky. If you fail, the dream junkies will absolutely destroy her," said Chief.

I had no answer to that. He was right. She was the one at risk who played little to no role of putting herself at risk.

"I think this Becky wouldn't have it any other way," Uncle Bennett boomed from the rear. "She bears our family mark. Which of you wouldn't take that risk for your family? And it's not only about Taven. She also needs rescuing because assuming she will be better off carved out from the family is also folly. And how do you know Taven isn't right? All we know about dreams and going into dreams and severing connections is what we've been told by..."

"Bennett," warned Chief.

I was surprised to see Uncle Bennett immediately refrain from whatever it was he was going to say. He didn't strike me as one who would be subject to the commands of another, but in this instance he certainly was. "What matters is there is almost always more than one way to solve a problem. And carving out Becky is a far greater harm to her personally than to try to rescue her from these fiends. I for one would be willing to fight them."

"As would I," said great grandma Toone, as nearly everyone in the crowd stepped forward, voicing their assent.

Chief's face was unreadable. I wasn't sure how things worked here, but if it was a democracy, we were going to get a chance to find out if our plan was going to work. Before the rumble of the crowd could subside on its own, Chief raised his hand and waited for everyone to sit in the same places within their groups. "Taven, maybe it was good you weren't named John after all," Chief began. I cringed at what I expected would come next, "because sometimes what is needed is something different. This Becky is one of us and I don't want to lose her. Your venture is worth the risk. And, believe it or not, I don't want to lose you either. You are more important than you realize."

Despite how badly I'd messed everything up, I was being given another chance, another chance to make things right. What was amazing about this second chance was that I was not being made to feel I was unworthy of it, rather the moment Chief had spoken, everyone in the crowd broke ranks and joined in congratulating me. In that moment, by experience, I began to understand what it meant to be connected.

Chief raised his hand again and all was quiet, although no one returned to their positions. "Taven and Finn, go and help Becky. It's almost nighttime and those villains are sure to strike. Bennett, my boy, I'll leave it to you to organize a group to check on the rest of the connections, to make sure they're okay. To make sure the dream junkies don't break way from their normal patterns."

"Yes, sir," replied Uncle Bennett. "Before you boys go," he began, turning back to us, "I need to talk to you about the shepherd boy. What amazes me about him is not what he has accomplished. In the scope of the world, his story will not be remembered. His daily walk is repetitive. But he is always happy. Although subject to all the normal emotions and the to and fro of mortality, he is balanced, he is stable, he is self-sufficient. He simply is." Uncle Bennett turned, and with a simple "Let's go" sped off, followed by the rest of the group, except Chief.

"Taven," Chief said, looking more fatherly than I ever remembered him, "things aren't always as they seem. I believe in you more than you know." And with that, he was gone.

On the offensive

I had been working on my Grade Seven project on the Russian revolution, worth thirty-three percent of my social studies mark, for two solid weeks. With my mom's help, I'd put together a colorful and informative poster and I'd run through the actual presentation enough times to have it memorized. But when the morning for presenting came, I didn't want to get out of bed. The thought of failure had drowned out all the preparation and that doubt remained with me through breakfast, on the bus ride, and as I sat in my desk. Arriving in Becky's bedroom, and seeing her in a restless sleep, I felt the same crippling anxiety in spite of what I knew.

From the time Chief left, to our arrival in the room where Becky lay sleeping, the suffocating power of the thought that I hadn't been successful the last two trips into her dreams increased. Standing in the bedroom, I no longer had any idea why I had felt so confident asserting I would be successful this time.

"You look sick. You do realize when you're dead you don't get sick anymore, don't you?" Finn said.

I wiped my forehead. "Just a little nervous."

Finn jovially smacked me on the back. I don't know how he was so cheerful when there was so much at stake. "There's nothing to be nervous about. If we fail, we're not in any worse position than we would have been had we not tried. So, no worries."

"Right. No worries," I replied, not nearly as enthusiastically as Finn had done.

"So what's the plan?" Finn asked as we stood there looking down at Becky sleeping.

Maybe that was why I was feeling more and more stressed. I still had no idea how I was going to rescue this little girl and save myself in the process. "My plan is... we'll... I guess we'll figure it out once we get in."

"Simple. Efficient. I like it. How do you want to... look at her face," said Finn. Becky looked like I felt when I was told I was going to be carved out. "No more time for planning. Get us in."

I put my hands on Becky's head. I motioned for Finn to grab my arm. "No need, brother. We're all connected. Besides, we're in this together." Finn placed his own hands directly on her head.

The darkness came. "Please leave me alone. Don't... I don't want you in here... Please I can't... I need help. Help me." I was embarrassed my little brother could hear her pleas for us to leave her alone.

His familiar voice cut the tension. "Don't worry little girl. We're not the bad guys. We're here to help."

Panic was evident in Becky's voice, "Please... please... leave me alone. Someone help me."

The voice faded as the darkness opened to the same courtyard Fiona had brought me to the first time.

"Dreary place." Finn whistled. He was right. The allure of the mansion and its surroundings was now gone. A black and decaying monstrosity of a house loomed over us, the menacing row of trees, almost daring us to walk down peered at us. The air was stiff and cold, the aroma was death. I wondered if it had looked the same the first time or if I had so been under Fiona's spell, so much subject to my own desires that I was blinded to where she was taking me and to what she was asking me to do. "This look familiar to you?"

"It does. Let's go. She was inside the house last time, in a room off of the main hallway," I said.

Side by side, my brother and I walked cautiously up the pathway until we came within a tree length of the ominous vegetation bordering the left and right sides of the path. Having been there before, I motioned for Finn to wait while I stepped forward on the path. Before I could take a second step, I was sent flying backwards. I forgot the pain shooting through my gut the instant I slammed crash dummy like, except with no car, into the large stone arch over the entry to the path.

Finn jogged to me. Extending his hand, he said, "Maybe we should try it together this time."

"Sure thing," I wheezed as he pulled me to my feet. The pain was real and intense, but the healing was perfect, complete and almost instant. "Okay, I'm ready."

"Run with me, brother."

"You got it... wait!" Finn was two steps in front of me. I caught up to him as we reached the threshold of the trees. I wasn't more than three steps in before I was being knocked around like a ball in a pinball machine, only to be ejected into a prickly bush back at the entrance. Assuming Finn would soon be joining me by way of tree-induced flight, I forced my eyes open. All I saw was a blurred Finn ducking and jumping, always one step ahead of the trees only he wasn't moving toward the house any more. He was nimbly making his way back to me.

"Are you okay?" he asked.

"I'm fine," I said, trying to stand gracefully but failing miserably. "How did you move like that?"

"I'm a hero remember," he announced.

I wasn't sure I remembered and I had no idea what to say to that. "No, really, tell me how to do what you did."

"It's because I am a hero," I opened my mouth but he motioned for me to close it. "Wait, listen. I think you spend too much time thinking about what you can't do. Everything I do. Everything I am. I act what I believe. I simply am what I believe myself to be. I think people spend so much time focusing on the negatives. They forget the fantastic things they've done. For sure negatives do harm, but focusing on them only compounds the problem. Focusing on the fantastic things, well, it gives less room for the negative ones." He paused and, putting his hand on my shoulder, said in his grandiose way, "Go with your instincts and you'll be fine."

"My instincts tell me I should let you go first." And I motioned for my little brother to go first. Without hesitation Finn sprinted at the trees. His clothing transformed, from the business suit, to a large flannel shirt, baggy blue jeans and suspenders. I wouldn't have been surprised if he sprouted a beard. Just before reaching the trees, a humungous axe appeared in his hands and with one mighty running swoop three trees on the right fell backward, completely severed from their trunks. Finn continued down the line hacking and slashing the trees on the right, every swing a smooth motion, blade passing through wood as though it was butter, leaving neither twig nor root that attempted to stop his progress.

"Are you coming?" he asked now standing to the right of the path at the steps into the house. I was so mesmerized by the power and grace of his onslaught, I'd never seen a lumberjack go to work with such pizzazz and flare, I had forgotten I was supposed to play a role in this rescue effort. With a little popcorn and pop, I could have watched that for another hour.

"I left the other side for you," he shouted.

"Where'd you get your axe? How did you change your clothes?"

Finn opened his mouth to speak, but was interrupted by a deep muffled groan that rumbled the ground. He yelled, "Hurry up."

I ran along the right side of the path, the trees on the left side able to swipe at but not make contact with me. Moving past Finn and to the door, I asked him, "Did you save anything for an encore?"

Despite turning the handle, the door seemed to cling to the frame. It too was resisting our entrance. I was feeling pretty useless at this point. "Why don't you chop through it?"

"I would, but I'm not sure what's on the other side. Besides, I'm sure we can get it together. Let's pull on the count of three." We both placed our hands on the doorknob. "One. Two. Three."

The force of our pulling was so great the door handle popped out of the door and we flew backward, landing at the bottom of the stairs: Finn, gracefully on his feet and me, flat on my back.

While I was picking myself off the ground, again, Finn rushed to the door, his clothes transforming into a beat up sweatshirt, florescent green Bermuda shorts and an orange hard hat. He attached a huge hook, which materialized the moment he threaded it through the hole in the door where the doorknob had been. A cord materialized from the hook and extended to the bumper of a large truck, the kind of truck you need a step to get into, with blazing red paint and lightning bolt decals, its tires up to my waist and engine roaring to deafening decibels.

Finn was off the step and into the truck almost before it had fully come into being. A second roar of the truck was followed by the immediate squeal of the tires, and a creak as the door was ripped from its hinges.

Standing at the bottom of the steps, I barely dodged the cord as it whipped by my face. "What else have you got in your pocket?"

Finn didn't answer. He jumped out of the truck, and ran to me and the house, grabbing my arm with so much force I was jolted along with him.

The interior of the house looked as though it had aged well beyond its usefulness. Floorboards were rotten, the staircase had collapsed, and the wallpaper was curled and blackened as though it had been burnt by fire. It smelled like a boy's locker room, if the room was ten times smaller and the boys were ten times sweatier. Surveying the space, Finn asked, "Where was she last time?"

"The door on the right of the hallway," I answered. "I'm going to wait here. You seem to know what you're doing and I'm just going to end up in the way."

"But you'll miss out on all the fun."

"You go ahead. I'll wait here. Call me... if you... you're probably not going to need me. Let me know when you find Becky."

"Are you sure?"

"Sure."

Finn shrugged and rushed for the door on the right of the hallway, which in turn sprinted away from us. The faster he went, the further it was from him and from me. Feeling like I had basically nothing to offer in the circumstances, I waited for Finn to come up with some kind of rocket car, high-speed bike, grappling hook or anything to get us in that door. But nothing changed, Finn kept chasing the door, never really catching up.

While watching him run, the idea occurred to me if we could slow it down, we could catch up to it. That idea was followed by the concept, almost tangible in my mind, that all I needed was a remote control.

"Taven, do something," shouted Finn.

"I don't know what to do?" I shouted back.

"Focus on whatever comes to mind," he shouted.

If what he wanted was a remote control, then I'd concentrate on a remote control. Seizing hold of the remote control idea, I focused on it and in my hand was a remote control with one button on it. My brother came up with the amazing axe of destiny and possibly the coolest truck I had ever seen in my life and I couldn't even come up with an interesting remote control. It was a one-buttoned sad-looking first-generation black box sorry excuse for a remote.

"What are you waiting for?" Finn yelled, the door almost out of sight.

I pressed the button and the fleeing door, the swinging and now useless hinges, even the dust in the air, everything in the house, with the exception of Finn and I, slowed beyond a crawl to a complete stop. Not only did everything stop, but, like an accordion retracts into itself, the distance between myself, Finn and the door was gone.

"Hurry, Taven," We scrambled through the door. It was a good thing we hurried as the slow motion effect ceased as we were entering the room. Taking with it the room's only light, the door whipped past us, leaving us in a blind darkness.

"Finn?" I called.

"I'm right here," he said, as he grabbed onto my arm. "Why did you hesitate?"

"I don't know. Wouldn't you have hesitated if the only thing you could come up with was a remote control?"

"Who said you came up with it?" he asked. "Where was she last time you were in this room?"

"She was against the back wall. How are we going to find her in the darkness?"

At the same time I would have expected an audible response, a tiny helicopter, with a mounted lamp that lighted an area just slightly in front of us, hovered overhead. Finn's shadowed face was pointed at the miniature machine. "Take us to her... Taven, keep up. I don't want to lose you. We don't have time to waste trying to find each other."

A muted weeping emerged as we edged forward, following our guide.

"Becky?" I called, staying close to Finn, and within the boundaries of the oval shaped illumination. I couldn't see her, but it sounded like her. "Becky?"

"Who's Becky?" a frightened young voice called out.

It was as though we were on one of those unbearably long scout hikes and I'd led Finn the wrong direction for three hours, only there was a lot more at stake than more walking. But we weren't going in the wrong direction, I knew that voice as well as I knew anything. "It sounds like her, but... is she confused?" I whispered to Finn. "Do you think this is a trap?"

"Only one way to find out," he responded. After a few more steps, he asked, "Have you considered the possibility her name isn't Becky?"

The reality was she had never told me what her name was. I hadn't seen it on a nameplate. "What made you think Becky wasn't her name?"

"Chief knows the entire family. He didn't know who Becky was but she's clearly part of the family. So I knew that wasn't her name," he said. "And the person you call Becky doesn't know who you're talking about."

The light of the helicopter stopped on a tiny huddled figure, nightgown pulled tightly around her legs.

"It's her." I hurried to her side and knelt in front of her. "Are you okay? We're here to rescue you."

"Help me," she screamed, as she crooked her head away from me.

"No. I'm here to help you. I can protect…"

Whistle-like, her voice pierced my eardrums and sent a chill up every nerve. Hoping Finn had a better idea, I turned to ask but he was gone. A light switch sprung to mind. Concentrating on it, it appeared on the floor. I flipped the switch and the room was bathed in light, the contrast from dark to light being so extreme that all I saw at first was a white blur. Gradually my vision returned. Finn was a great distance from me, far enough I couldn't influence what was happening. He was face to face with a great living mound of grey, brown and green muck, which was jellyfish like in its movements. More than ten times his size, it slid to him, bulging as though it threatened to swallow him up.

"Watch out!" I screamed.

Having gathered into a tight mass, the gigantic beast propelled itself into the air and over the top of my little brother. The massive bulk of the thing crashed over him, flattening out completely and rippling the floorboards to where I was charging, causing me to stumble. The monster drew itself back into a mound.

"Finn!" I shouted. The beast rumbled in the same tone I'd heard before, only this time I was sure it was mocking me. Before I could get to it, it rotated its massive girth on the spot, like a foot scrubbing out the embers of the cigarette beneath it. Only the cigarette was Finn. Strength, pure strength, came to mind and I concentrated on it. My shirt seemed to tighten around my neck, chest and arms as I charged at an increased speed.

The gargantuan slug crouched and again bounded into the air. Everything was happening so fast, but in a way, it was also very slow. There was enough time for me to scan the ground for the squashed remnants of my brother, which weren't there. There was enough time for me to raise my arms in preparation for impact. There was enough time for me to decide that I no longer cared whether I lived or died so long as I could somehow rescue my brother and the little girl.

The slimy undercarriage first touched my outstretched hands then folded over the rest of my body. Despite its immense size, its mass had no effect on me. With small effort I swept both of my arms forward and sent the gelatinous blob hurtling, the creature rotating, extensions reaching out as though to grab anything to stop its trajectory, the whole splatting against the wall, great parts exploding from the main body.

"Help!" screamed the girl.

I turned to see a hulking figure bathed in shadow in the midst of the light.

"What are you waiting for? Go help her." A shining blade sliced through the exterior of the glob, opening a hole large enough for Finn to leap out.

"I'm coming!" I rushed toward the little girl and the tall creature. As I came closer, I could tell it was at least four times my height and had the basic shape of a person, but its arms hung stiffly all the way to the floor. It had a long narrow head that drooped forward, as though there was a weight on the very tip of it. Flame-like, the edges of the shadowy creature danced in the light but was neither penetrated nor dispersed by the light.

"Stay away from me! Get away from me!" The little girl backed away from the slow and steady approach of the nightmare.

The idea of jumping came to mind. No sooner had seized on the concept, I leapt and was between the shadowy creature and the girl. "Get back."

The girl sprinted backwards. And just in time because the creature raised its right arm and chopped in my direction, narrowly missing me owing to a step to the left at the last possible moment. The floorboards splintered under the force of the blow. I grabbed the creature's arm, determined to prevent another attack, but it lifted me up into the air. I hung upside down about five times my height from the floor.

Great shears came to mind and they were soon in hand. I released the arm only to land on the back of what I assumed was the head, but now that I was so close, more resembled a roll of material than anything else. I shuffled up to the tip of what I thought was the head, and with both hands gripped firmly onto what was in fact a roll of carpet. I cut the twine wrapped around the top of the roll and pulled with all my might and weight, causing the long creature to lose its balance and fall to the floor with a bang.

The little girl shrieked as we landed within a short distance from her.

"Don't worry," I said, "I'll show you what this guy is made of." Running to the middle of the shadowy carpet beast, I blew as hard as I could, and to my surprise, the shadow dispersed revealing massive rolls of carpet, seemingly fixed together with duct tape. Running to the seams, I cut through the tape with the shears and kicked the roll, unrolling the carpet, which began in a straight line but no sooner did I imagine it covering the room than it covered the entire room with a comfortable plush carpet. Even the corner where Finn was tormenting a much smaller blob with his sword was covered.

I hadn't noticed the little girl had walked up to me, "Thank you for helping me."

"I've been calling you Becky all along. Pretty silly of me to get it wrong all this time. What is your name?" I asked, holding a hand out to her to help her up.

The girl hesitated for a moment, as though she was working out whether I was someone she could trust with such an important piece of information, but deciding suddenly, she placed her hand in mine and turned those great blue orbs on me. "My name is Eve."

Memory overpowered the sensations of the dream and those same eyes shone on me in very different circumstances. We were in the same baseball field I was last in with the dream junkies, only the sky was a majestic blue, painted with pristine cumulous clouds, the grass a vibrant living green, the ball diamond was populated by batters and pitchers and catchers and fielders, and I was at my vending cart, not far away and not alone. I stood next to the girl of my dreams.

"Did you get in much trouble with the police?" Eve asked.

"No, they let me off with a ticket and a warning," I said. I had forgotten about this conversation. I thought the whole swerving into traffic was the end of our friendship. But this was memory. I knew it was. There was a certainty about it. A reality to it.

"Just a warning, eh? They probably should have thrown you in jail. Smarten you up a bit," she said.

"Maybe. It probably would have been better than paying the ticket," I said.

"How much was your ticket?" she asked, placing her hand the handle of my cart.

"Two hundred and fifty dollars," I said. She gasped. "I know. That's about two-hundred and fifty hot dogs before I make any profit again."

"I didn't know you could get a ticket for stalking somebody," she said with a smile.

"I wasn't stalking... I was... no... you know... it was for stunting," I sputtered. I was so embarrassed that she knew the reason we were near her house.

"Oh. That's not what Carl said. But it makes sense that it wouldn't be for stalking because it can't be stalking if the person being stalked wants the person to come over," she said, stepping closer to me.

"You wanted me to come to your house? I wish I would have known. It would have saved me a lot of money. I'm going to be stuck here for the foreseeable future," I said, motioning to the grill of my stand.

"I could keep you company," she said, now right next to me.

"Really?" I asked, feeling like I'd won the lottery.

"My younger brothers play most nights anyway, so it wouldn't be hard for me to come." She turned me from the grill to her with a gentle tug at my shoulder. "I like being around you, Taven."

"Really?" I asked.

"The only reason I didn't say yes to you the other night was I had promised my friends I'd hang out with them," she explained, dispelling the last of my reasons for disbelief.

"Really?" I asked again.

"Well, and I didn't want to be seen associating with a criminal," she said with a laugh.

I didn't laugh. I mentally urged the seventeen year-old me to laugh, but I understood why I didn't. My most secret desire, my fondest dream, my great hope had been realized without fanfare and naturally, like dew on the grass in the morning, and I was busy internally pinching myself.

She looked concerned. "I was only joking, Taven."

I grabbed her hands. "I know. I just…"

"If you're not interested that's…"

"I am interested!" I shouted, startling her enough that she looked as though a gust of wind had caught her breath. I continued, more in control of myself, "I've been dreaming about this for a long time."

"You've been dreaming of me…" I felt like I'd been grabbed under my armpits and lifted from my first person's perspective of Eve's beautiful face to a bird's eye view of she and I contentedly speaking to each other. A blinding pain in my shoulder and piercing scream, shocked me back to the dream and my present. I was back in the large, pink-carpeted room, only now I was hanging high above the much younger and screaming Eve.

My shoulder was pierced by shining metal blades. A massive creature held me in the air. Cactus-like, it was covered, from tip to toe in rusted, metal knives.

I cut my hands when I grabbed the finger blades that pierced my shoulder, that tore at my body when I struggled to be released and sliced my legs when I kicked against the arm. I wanted to cry out for help, but panicking would only make things worse for Eve. As it was, she looked moments away from a complete breakdown, she sobbed uncontrollably and gripped at her hair as though tugging on it would somehow transport her out of this place.

The deadly fingers began to close, slicing further into my shoulder. I thought I could feel the claws driving into my bones, threatening to snap them.

"Let him go!" Finn swung a long gnarled wooden stick. The impact made the beast stumble and loosen its grip on me momentarily. That was when a hard foam ball came to mind, which was in an instant in my hands. I immediately shoved the foam into palm of the hand of the monster, and with great effort, pushed on the foam ball until the fingers were forced out of my shoulder, at which point I released the ball and fell to the ground.

I landed on my back. The creature turned on Finn and cut through his stick with a slash of its other arm, causing him to stumble and lose his balance.

I scurried to my feet, the pain in my shoulder overwhelming. "Finn, are you alright?" No sooner had I spoken than the creature pivoted on me, swinging the same bladed hand that had sliced the stick. A pincushion sprung to mind, and was in my hands in time to protect myself from the blades. The creature spread its fingers, shredding the fabric and leaving me unprotected.

"No, you don't!" Costumed like a firefighter, Finn stood behind the creature with hose in hand. The creature raised its hand to strike me but was frozen in mid-swing by what must have been specially formulated extra rust-inducing water.

Having disabled the metallic monstrosity, Finn turned off his hose and ran to me, his clothes transforming into doctor's scrubs. He applied a compress to my shoulder, which instantly removed the pain and healed the wound. "Nice muscles... Next time you try to rescue me, can you be a little more gentle? The slam against the wall hurt me more than the giant goober did."

I looked at my chest. It wasn't until that moment that I realized that my body had transformed into a Mr. Olympian type physique that was stretching the capacity of my shirt. I couldn't resist a bicep flex. "I think my bicep is bigger than my head."

"Is that even possible?"

"What's that supposed to mean?"

"Taven?"

Finn looked perplexed. "Becky doesn't look very good."

"Her name is Eve and no she doesn't." I had forgotten how close she was to the fighting. It was a miracle she didn't get hit. Five steps and I was next to her. Her head hung deeply between her knees and a depressive aura hung about her. I sat next to her and put my hand gently on her shoulder. "Are you hurt? You're safe. We saved you."

Hesitantly the girl lifted her head. "Are you okay?"

"I'm fine. See, my shoulder works great. Finn, fixed me right up." After everything she'd been through, her first question was about me. This had to be her. "Do we know... I mean... I know you're a little girl but I've been dreaming about an older version of you..."

Finn elbowed me in the side. "This sounds weird. Are you sure about where you are going with this? Eve, will you excuse us for a second?"

Eve nodded. Finn and I walked to the other side of the rusted monster.

"But I have been dreaming about... no, not dreaming, remembering a girl named..."

"Let's discuss this when the little girl is not at the point of a breakdown. Do you realize how creepy this would sound to her... how it sounds to me?"

"You're right. But... you're right."

"I know." He abruptly turned from me and with the relationship building skill of a long-running television game show host, pulled me back to Eve and said, "That's Taven, I'm Finn. We came to rescue you and we did. You don't have to be afraid anymore."

"Thanks, but I still feel afraid," Eve said, trembling. Semi-shielding what she was doing, she pointed at me. "and that guy keeps getting beat up in all my dreams."

"It's because I'm trying to help you," I burst in.

"What if you can't?" she asked.

"I... I know I can," I said.

"They almost killed you. They're going to get me," she moaned.

"They can't kill me," I said, hoping that was the truth.

Eve shook her head violently. "But it was so scary. I can't do it. It's too hard. I don't want to have these scary dreams..."

Whatever else Eve said was drowned out in the deafening grinding of metal against metal. Before we could move out of the way, the massive rusted spiked and metal creature fell on top of us. Eve's scream echoed in my ears as we were sucked up and out of the dilapidated mansion and into Eve's room in the mortal world. I didn't feel the spikes enter my body, but I wondered if she had.

We entered into the room as though in reverse, the first thing I saw as we entered the room was Eve's tormented face. Finn and I landed at the foot of her bed, a little more than an arm's length from Fiona, Ben and Dan. Fiona looked strangely calm. It seemed like I should have felt hatred from her, and in my imagination I did, but that wasn't it at all. Ben and Dan looked as though they were being physically restrained from attacking us.

Eve's mother opened the door to her room. "Sweetheart, are you alright? We heard you screaming."

A gasp for breath, the kind that always follows a thorough crying, was the only answer.

The mother entered the room and knelt next to her bed. She gently stroked her hair. She quietly whispered, "I don't know what's going on the last few days but I want you to know I love you. You are an amazing girl. Things will be alright."

The pained look had diminished somewhat. The mother stroked Eve's hair one last time, allowing her hand to rest on her back, then stood and left the room, concern etched on her face.

"You need to leave her alone," I said.

"Failing as a hero again?" Fiona's words stung but I felt no animosity from her.

"Were you a seamstress in another life? Did you really conjure up a pin cushion?" Ben taunted, sounding as if he was a grizzly bear that had learned how to communicate in English.

"You are only speeding our work along. The sad part for you is even if you could stop us, and you can't, we can destroy your entire family and there isn't a thing you can do about it. You're on your own. You can't do a thing about it. There won't be much left for the master to... ravage." When Dan spoke, his words were accompanied by a venomous feeling that bit more than what he said.

"You're wrong about that. I am going to stop you," I said.

"Big words from a guy who can't even save one little girl," snorted Ben.

"I know who you devils are," said Finn.

Before I could react, Fiona grabbed Finn's hand. "Do you?"

Finn blinked and pulled his hand away. "Yes, I do."

"Good for you. Who's this, Taven? Your baby brother? Did you bring him along to fix your booboos?" Fiona said as she paced in front of Ben and Dan. She stopped next to Dan and placed her hand on his shoulder. "Maybe we can teach Taven a lesson through his brother. Don't you think, Dan?"

It was as though Dan's bonds had been cut. No longer restrained, he lunged at Finn and planted his hand into his chest. The impact sent Finn flying backwards into the wall where he remained.

"Finn, are you alright?" I asked as I knelt next to my lifeless brother.

Dan was nearly hysterical. "You can't stop us. You can come into the dreams and fight all you want. We're having a great time with it. Maybe next time we'll sever a limb, or put out an eye or kill you. So, please keep coming. She'll always be scared and it's only a matter of time before she gives up."

"Maybe you're the one who'll end up dead, Dan," I growled.

"Can't die if you never lived," replied Fiona. "It's not like you Taven to be so vindictive. This is all just a game."

I looked at my unconscious brother on the floor. "How is doing this in your best interest? How is hurting my brother, how is tormenting that little girl, how is tormenting me in your best interest?"

Fiona came within whispering distance of me "You'll just have to trust me that it is." She touched my arm and backed away. "Dan, Ben, do what you do. Bye, Taven."

The next moments were a blur: Fiona vanished, Ben and Dan lunged at me, and, knowing they couldn't do Eve any more harm now that the dream was over, I grabbed Finn's arm. While drawing the park in my mind, I felt a sharp fiery jab in my side which expanded into a flaming torment beyond anything I had experienced before.

Building immunity

Tortured, no longer aware of either surrounding or self, I writhed in the burnings of lost opportunity, failed expectation, regret and what felt like physical pain. I saw, heard and felt nothing but the sensations associated with bruises, broken bones, scraped flesh, disease, embarrassment, impending doom, everything unpleasant from life I wished would have stayed buried, but the rotten corpses of bitter experience emerged from what should have been impenetrable tombs. At that moment extinction seemed a happy alternative to this tormented state, which seemed to have no end.

But a light pierced the gloomy cloudiness of my personal pit of torment. Dimly at first, but comprehensible to me, a memory of Eve dawned, not the little girl, but the one from my hot dog cart. The rays of hope effected a recession of what had seemed to be the relentless tides of hurt. Remembering her was warm, comfortable and healing. I awoke.

I was lying on my side facing a lifeless Finn. We were next to the path that ran through the middle of the field. It was a brilliant morning in the mortal version of my park. "Finn, are you alright?"

Finn did not respond. The living people ran by ignorant of my fear for the loss of my brother and what we had passed through. But I was all too aware of them. Each runner that tromped by magnified the fact that despite being among so many we were alone and without help. Placing my hand on Finn's side, I unfocused and we shifted into the blurry alternate world.

"It's me. Taven," I said with my hand still on his shoulder, feeling the warmth of his love for me and my love for him, which was intermittently displaced by the deadly frost of the realization of loss. "Wake up!"

He didn't respond. A thousand thoughts ran through my mind. I wondered if he was dead again or annihilated or if he was just paralyzed. Losing my brother a second time was not something I had ever fathomed dealing with. But he couldn't be dead again. I somehow knew he would be alright despite what I was seeing. The temporary relief of this assurance did not prevent the flood of other problems. How I could stop Fiona, Ben and Dan from tormenting Eve, from tormenting others in my family. Was this little girl really the Eve? Had I somehow transported into the past? Were my memories actually predictions of the future?

"You look stressed out," said Finn, propped up on one elbow and clearly amused by my state of being. "If you don't relax your face might stay that way."

I leapt to my feet and pulled my brother to his. "You're okay! I thought you were dead."

Looking at me as though I'd told him the sky was green, he said, "I am dead."

"Right," I said.

"Just so you know. You only die once," he explained.

"I know but that doesn't mean I can't be excited when it works out," I said. "What happened back there?"

"As soon as Dan touched me, I didn't know what was going on any more. I was launched into the most terrible stream of memories, none of them good. The time I flushed Dad's watch down the toilet, the time I ate Mom's deodorant, the time I smeared my diaper on the wall; it wasn't so much what I did, but an intensified feeling of disappointment because there was no way I could fix the things I'd done wrong. I couldn't change the fact that I was a failure. But it was more than that, it was like a getting a shot of concentrated pain. Talking about it brings it back. Right here," he said, pointing to his chest. "Even now I feel it gripping at me, trying to draw me back in."

"What made it stop?" I asked.

"Your voice," he said. "When I heard your voice, you sound like Dad, you know, I remembered the fun times: Dad laughing as he wrestled with us, Mom holding me in her arms as she sang to me. I remembered the fun times we've had here, our adventures."

I smiled. And then I remembered. "Even those things you think were bad, were so important to us. It seemed like Mom didn't smile or laugh for a long time after you died. I found out later that she felt like if she laughed, it was somehow a demonstration that you didn't mean anything to her. That she'd forgotten you. But it didn't stay that way. I clearly remember sitting at the dinner table a few weeks after you had died when little Karen started talking about the crazy things you used to do, the things you thought were so bad. I watched her wondering if she was going to get in trouble or if Mom would start crying. After a moment or two of silence, Mom smiled and started to laugh. Then Dad told us some stories about some of the things you had done we had never heard before, like that you used to wait for us at the window, screaming our names and giggling, when we came home from school. We all laughed and felt at peace for the first time in a long time. Sharing your experiences opened our hearts to what we'd been hoping all along; that we would see you again. Turns out we were right."

Finn embraced me and lifted me off the ground. "Thank you, Taven. I feel so much better. In fact, if Dan were to try touching me again, I think knowing what you told me will be like a shield to whatever he might do."

"I think you might be on to something. Umm... you can put me down now," I said. Once back on the ground, I asked, "Tell me why it is you think it will act as a shield?"

"Because here, you're only affected by what you allow to affect you. I didn't resist the memories because I guess deep down, I always had a nagging doubt. Listening to you, helped me to realize I'd been too hard on myself, so next time I'll remember that and resist the memories," he said, as he walked to our rock skipping place.

"Next time will be different," I said, matching his pace. As we walked, for the first time, this alternate world, though not like the other, though not so brightly colored, was beautiful to me. I found solace in its melancholy, strength in its calm. On our approach to the edge of the water, he grabbed me and we were back in the mortal world. It was no longer strange to me to travel this way. At the water's edge, I said, "Her name is Eve."

Finn hesitated, then asked "Who?"

"Becky," I said. "Becky is Eve."

He looked relieved. "Great. It's good we know her real name." He was instantly far more interested in the imaginary stone in his hand than in the significance of who this was.

"Eve, Finn," I said fully expecting him to comprehend why this was a notable piece of information.

Finn tossed the stone, counting the imaginary skips across the top of the water. "Okay?"

"I've been dreaming about this girl, not the little girl, but a more grown up version ever since I got here," I said, following Finn into the river. He happily watched the fish swim past. "Now that I'm saying it out loud, I don't even know if it really happened before. But I keep seeing her in my memories, she's the one who pulled me out of the pain. This is the girl I had the biggest crush on... that... that... I would have married if I had the chance. I saw her tonight but she was little. She was Becky. It was her. That must have been why I was so drawn to the house."

"Are you sure?" He said walking past me and back to the bank. "There are, as you informed me, billions of people in the world."

I scurried out after him. "I know it sounds crazy but it's not just the looks. It's the feeling I get when I look at her. It's like she's a part of me. It's not like I can do anything about it now. Is it possible we are in the past? Like were we in the past, when I was a little kid and she was a little kid? If I looked hard enough could I find myself?"

Finn stood on the bank, shaking the water off as if he needed to. "The way I understand it you can only observe what happens in the past, and what we did tonight was a lot more than observing. But I don't understand everything. We could ask the family."

"No, we can't. We haven't fixed a thing and the dream junkies know what we're up to. We've got to make things right first," I said.

"Right," he said, picking up another stone.

"How did you know Fiona?" I asked, picking up my own imaginary stone. Strangely enough, when I did, it felt I was actually holding stone, not really felt, but remembered what it was like. I tossed it and in my mind saw the splash in the river. It was like the experience was a collage of my memories.

"Is Fiona another girl you're in love with? You've got to pull yourself together, Taven," he said.

"No, it was the woman in Becky's... I mean Eve's bedroom," I said.

Finn dropped his imaginary stones on the ground and brushed off his hands. "I didn't know her. But I recognized what she could be."

"What do you mean?" I said, throwing another stone into the water.

"There are two basic types of people here, Taven. Those who lived and then died, and those who died before they ever lived." He motioned for me to follow him back to the clearing.

I followed, perplexed by yet another new piece of information that would have been helpful in advance of meeting Fiona, Ben and Dan. "What's the difference?"

"There are plenty of differences but the main difference is there is a chance to help most of the people who have lived and died. Especially the ones who never really had chance to learn what it is to be happy while they were alive. They can choose to make a course correction and learn to be happy before they move on." Finn paused. "That's what I do. I help. I find people who are sad, and help them to learn to be happy."

"What about the ones who never lived?" I asked.

Finn slowly closed his eyes and exhaled. "The ones who never lived... can't be helped. It's possible the dream junkies are that kind of people. Not sure how it all worked out, but they were never alive and so never learned to live. They hate everything that took on life and seek to destroy all advantages of living."

In spite of everything she had caused, at that moment I pitied Fiona. "Why can't they be helped?"

"Because the way things are set up, the way things are, are contrary to what they have chosen to be. They are a contradiction to things as they really are, so they are never satisfied. The fleeting pleasure they get is from knocking someone else out of course, to join them in their state of contradiction. Misery is what they chose… death is what they chose without ever tasting life." Finn and I arrived at the park. He sat on a swing. I stood next to him.

"Is there any hope? Are we wasting our time?" I asked.

"Taven, I've been counting on you for that. You said there was hope, and I believed you. And I still do. So, no, I don't believe we are wasting our time. And even if we were, Eve sounds like she is more than worth any effort we can give, whether we succeed," Finn paused as he pointed his feet behind him, as if he could make the swing move, "or we fail.".

"So what are we going to do? How are we going to stop them?" I asked.

"I'm not sure we can stop them, big brother. I believe in you, but I don't know what to do. I'm following your lead here," he said. He leapt off the swing, it having been propelled gently by the wind, and stood beside me.

Finn was still dressed in the doctor's smock from the dream. I thought he looked like he'd come straight out of a costume shop from one of the malls downtown. Downtown. "There was a man, when I was downtown, that was able to hurt people by touching them. Maybe we could talk to him. Convince him to help us out. Fight fire with fire."

"I'm not so sure about using the whole, we're going to force you or trap you technique here. Even if it does work, pain is never a long-term fix to a problem. Especially with Fiona, she is already in pain," he said. Whether he caught me smirking at his doctor's outfit or it was the talk of fire, he instantly changed back into fireman's outfit, only he wasn't wearing the large fireproof overcoat.

I said, "You said you'd trust me, so trust me. I'm not sure how it will all work out and what we will gain from this, but it's the best and frankly only plan I have right now."

"Maybe you're right. I'm not on board with hurting the dream junkies to scare them into stopping because I don't think that will work, but maybe by knowing how to hurt them we can figure out a way of stopping them," he said. "We've got to pay attention so we know when Eve's going to sleep again. We can't afford to be the second ones into her dream this time. We need to take control of the dream."

Is there some type of special watch we can use?" I asked.

"Taven, Taven, Taven. You think this girl is the love of your life and you can't feel when she went to sleep? When she was scared? Our family connection gives us a way of protecting each other against harm. When Eve falls asleep we'll know. We're tuned into her signal, and we won't miss it," he said.

"Are you sure?" I asked.

Finn put his hand on my shoulder. "I found you, didn't I?"

"You did. We should get going," I said, as I drew the entrance to the downtown mall in my mind.

We instantly stood within a darkened hallway lit only by pale yellow lights. The gates in front of the shops were all down and the space devoid of human inhabitant. "I guess it's closed."

"Let's go outside and check," said Finn as he grabbed my wrist, whisking us to the sign on the outside of the mall indicating the doors opened every day at nine o'clock am. The electronic billboard across the street announced the time as eight fifty-three.

"What should we do now?" I asked.

"Grab my wrist," he said. I obeyed and was swept to the top of the building across the street from the mall entrance, which had to be at least thirty stories high. "Come with me," he said sprinting towards a cluster of birds. "Hang on to their legs. It is awesome."

Wondering whether other heroes spent the few moments of their free time in a similar way, I crouched down beside the pigeon and grasped its legs. "Shouldn't we be working on a way to help Ev... ah," I screamed as the bird leapt off the edge and took flight. Dead or not, heights were never my thing. Suspended thirty stories in the air with nothing but air between me and the blocked off street below, hundreds and hundreds of people streaming like ants, was not my idea of a fun way to pass seven minutes. The pigeon flew directly for the ledge on the building across the street and landed, leaving me no place to stand, sit or crouch. I dangled from the side of the building from a pigeon's legs. Still in mid-air, Finn was hooting and hollering, clinging to the legs of his pigeon, which, much to his delight, chose a longer path of flight.

Back on the ground, people were starting to file into the mall. "Finn... Finn... It's nine. Are you coming?"

He disappeared almost before I could finish the sentence. Glad to be leaving this pigeon's perch, I drew the hallway in my mind and joined him in the now fully lit mall. I motioned to Finn, who was standing in front of the specialty popcorn shop, enthralled by the poster of the cartoon squirrel handing out multi-colored popcorn. "Have you ever had this popcorn? It looks so awesome. Look at the squirrel. It makes the popcorn."

"Finn. Come over here," I said.

Taking one last long look at the poster, Finn joined me across the hallway from the woman's shoe store. "Did you see that popcorn?"

"Yep. Pretty neat." We watched as the store employees trickled in, each opening their respective store gate, switching on the interior store lights and busying themselves in prepping the store for customers.

The same aggressive man with the visor, Elmer, entered the mall and took his place next to the woman's shoe store. "There he is," I said, counting it to our advantage that he was alone. I approached him, with Finn at my side.

Stomping toward me with his fist cocked, Elmer did not look happy to see me, which I thought was weird since he always seemed to get the better of our encounters. But I guess things didn't go his way with Fiona. "You think I hurt you last time? What? Did you think this firefighter was gonna be able to protect you? You're gonna need a lot more than a firefighter after what I do to you this time."

"Who peed in his corn flakes?" Finn whispered to me.

I held my ground, but held my hands up. "Whoa. I didn't come here looking for a fight. You've got a special talent. I'm interested to know how you do it. I might have something to trade that is worth your while."

"Kid. You ain't got nothin' worth my while unless you're joining my game. I don't care about no special talent. The only good a talent is, is to keep people in line. Otherwise, I could care less about it. The only reason I don't give my power away is I don't want nobody using it on me. The only thing that matters to me is my game because it is the only thing that's uncertain around here. Everything else is so predictable. Nothing changes. It's the unexpected I value. Like, say, this," he said as he struck me in the face.

It was like I'd been struck by a baseball bat, not physically, but by memory, and venom-like its devastation quickly spread to the various parts of my body. The pain of past hurts. The pain of rejection. Supreme among the pain was the idea that Eve had rejected me. That I had lost her forever and it was my fault. But I had the antidote. I knew I had a choice at that point, I could believe the message of pain or I could believe the last memory, that Eve had not rejected me, that our not being together was not my fault and that there was hope that we could be together again.

I chose to hope and with it the pain dissipated and everything in the hallway came back into view.

"Tough guy, eh?" he asked as he struck me in the midsection and again across the face.

Though excruciating at first, the effect of his attack was greatly minimized. It was as though I was developing a emotional callous.

Seeing that I was still standing, he struck me repeatedly. "What are you? Some kind of demon?"

The more he hit, the less impact there was to his touch until I was no longer affected at all by his touch. When he backed up, I spoke. "I think we've established that your special power isn't working anymore. You've given your best so why don't we sit down and talk things through?"

"My best? My best hasn't got anything to do with it. How about a serving of my worst?" the visored man said as he slammed his fist into Finn's chest.

Finn stumbled a bit at first, but quickly straightened. "I'm sorry bro. I've got it figured it out too. You seem really mad about something."

The man stepped back from us, rubbing his fist as though he'd injured it when he hit us. "Maybe you boys do have something I want, pretty valuable knowing how not to get hurt like that."

"Especially if we were to tell the people you play with how to do it," I said.

"Why would you do that? That won't do you no good," the man said.

"Why wouldn't we?" asked Finn. "Why would we allow you to continue bullying other people. You've got no hold on anybody other than by your power to intimidate. You've really got to calm down, dude. There are lots of better ways to bind someone to you, to bring them to your cause, to help them see it your way, and bullying isn't the way to do it."

The enraged man struck Finn again; Finn stood unfazed and unharmed, with an unshakeable look of determination on his face.

"The reason you're going to tell us your secret is because if you don't, we'll tell all those guys you play with," I said. "and you won't be able to hurt them anymore."

Elmer laughed. "You think these guys will figure it out? It ain't about just telling someone how to do a thing. What you guys got is pretty unique. I'll give you that. But givin' it to someone else ain't that simple. Besides, even if you do, and even if they are able to figure it out, you're just telling me, cause I'll make the same deal with them. I can find new guys to play with. These guys ain't like you. They are like me," he said as he pointed to the group of men, slowly walking towards the store, their voices reaching us.

"I can't believe you guessed it, yesterday. That was one in a million," said one man.

"Yah, who'd have thought the old guy who bought women's shoes was headed down to the fifteenth park bench along the river to try them on," said another. The group laughed.

"I know, and that I guessed it. My lucky day. If I keep it up, Elmer's going to tell me and then I'll set up my own game. With my own rules," said the last man in the group.

"Come on, boys," Elmer whispered, "give me your secret and I'll give you mine."

"Finn. Let's go."

"But…"

"I'll explain. Let's go."

"Alright. Let me know if you guys change your mind. I'm always here." Not wanting to hear any more of this pathetic man's words, I grabbed Finn's sleeve and in a moment we were next to the squirrel's tree.

"Why didn't we tell those other men?" Finn asked clearly upset. "At least we'd protect them from Elmer."

"Would you mind changing before we continue? Unless you have a fire to put out," I asked.

"Fine," said Finn, now dressed in orange tights with a large black 'F' on his torso.

"You know you look like a jack-o-lantern," I said.

"Why are you making jokes about me? There was someone doing bad and we didn't stop him from doing it, when we could have stopped him."

"Are you sure we would have stopped him? If we would have tried it would have been worse," I said. "And he was right. What we have, I don't think you can just give it."

"What do you mean?" Finn asked.

"It's like a present that you've got to put together before you play with it. Us telling those guys how would be like giving them the unassembled gift. I'm not sure they were in a place where they'd be able to put it together yet." I continued, "And even if they were able to do it, if we told those men how to resist Elmer's strength, the only way Elmer could have control over them would have been to tell them how to hurt others. Rather than there being one Elmer, there would have been many. I'm not willing to take that risk because it is very possible that those men were only different from Elmer because they didn't know how to do what Elmer knew how to do yet. You know birds of a feather..."

"Like birdseed?" Finn opened his mouth and then closed it. "You're right. Do I really look like a pumpkin?"

"No, I was just trying to get you to lighten up a little," I said.

"It's fine, Taven. I figured you were jealous." He ran his hands along the side of the outfit as though he were modeling it. "I think this outfit accentuates my manly physique."

"To each his own. Tights aren't really my thing. Besides, you are not quite as buff as I was in the dream."

"You looked like you were on steroids. I don't want to be that big. Au natural for me," he said, flexing his quadriceps.

The squirrel leapt from the tree to my shoulder, a warmth of companionship streaking from the point of impact. "Hi there, squirrelly. Were you worried about us?"

"Her name is ..." Finn proceeded to emit a squirrel like sound that had no resemblance to English.

"You mean..." All I wanted was to say this squirrel's name in appreciation for her kindness, her companionship with me when I so needed it, and to my surprise, the same squirrel-like noises came from my mouth. The squirrel, in response, leapt three times on my shoulder, then back into the tree and out of sight.

"When did you start speaking squirrel?" Finn asked.

"Just now..." I was interrupted by the squirrel that jumped back out of the tree and before I could protest, shoved an acorn in my mouth.

"Thank you," I mumbled in the squirrel tongue, the acorn filling a large portion of my mouth. Turning to Finn, I asked, "Where did she get the acorn and how did she pick it up?"

Finn was busy motioning for the squirrel to bring him an acorn. "Don't ask me? She's got all sorts of things figured out. She's taught me most of what I know how to do in this place."

"Wow," I spit the acorn into my hand expecting to be able to hold it, but my hand bent back under its weight. The acorn fell to the ground.

"Yah, she's definitely an awesome squirrel." Finn stared at the acorn on the ground for a few seconds, then looked back at me. "So, did we waste our time downtown?"

"Not at all. We learned two things . That you were right and that knowing how to protect ourselves is better than striking out. And that's what we can do to help Eve." No sooner had I finished speaking than almost imperceptibly I felt the sound of a chord played on the upper range of the piano.

"Did you feel that, Taven?" Finn asked.

"Feel what?" I asked.

"Eve," he said. "Can you feel her sound?"

Now that I was listening carefully for it, not so much with my ears but with my feelings, the chord increased in volume and intensity. "How do you know that's Eve? The family's got to be huge."

"It's the same sound I felt from her when we entered into her dream. It feels familiar, it feels right," he said.

He was right. The tone was calm and sure, rich and full. It resonated within me, and for a moment it seemed to be in harmony, sweet and tender, with my own sound. "It's beautiful."

"Whatever you want to call it, we need to get going. This time I'll drive," he said as he grabbed my arm.

We were instantly in a classroom, filled by twenty or so desks seating boys and girls, and a teacher at the front scribbling on the chalkboard. In the furthest corner from the front of the class, Eve sat slumped in her desk, her head in her hands, blank expression on her face.

"She does not look good," whispered Finn.

"No, she doesn't," I said, not lowering my voice at all.

A woman hovering over a boy toward the front turned to me and put her finger over her lips. "Shhh."

"Maybe it's just a really boring class," I said.

The woman took two steps to us. "No, she hasn't always been this way and I've been doing my best to coax her out of her malaise. If you are done interrupting the class, please leave."

"Did she say Eve's in mayonnaise?" Finn asked.

"No, she…"

"You can leave if you are going to be disruptive."

"Sorry," I said. "But how can you hear us?"

The woman marched for Finn and I, grabbed us both by the ears, which surprisingly to me, she was able to do and marched us out of the classroom. Once outside she spoke again, "If you can't show some respect for these students, you can sit in the hallway." With that she turned from Finn and I, and began checking the papers on the students desks as though we'd never been there.

"That was weird," said Finn.

"You're telling me. How did she know we were there?" I asked.

"I don't know. Only one way to find out." Finn leapt back into the classroom, put his hands up to his ears, stuck out his tongue and sang, "Nah, nah, nah, nah, nah, nah, you can't get me because I'm dead."

The woman at the chalkboard did not respond in the least. Neither did any of the students in the classroom. The lady checking papers whipped around to face Finn, and with a stare that could have melted ice cream, she put one finger over her lips and pointed with the other hand for the door. Finn turned and walked out of the room. "That was awesome. I've never been in school. Now I have. I'd never been in a class before. Now I have. And now I've been kicked out of one two times! Too cool."

"There's more to school than that. You forgot the whole learning part. Besides, we're here for Eve."

"We did learn something. That lady in there, the one who got me in trouble, she can either see dead people, or she's dead too. My bet's on dead. Nobody seemed to notice her shushing me."

The woman at the chalkboard, presumably the teacher, turned from the chalkboard, "Stephen Jenkins, kindly tell us the year of Canada's confederation."

The boy stood. The other woman, the stern one, raced from the row she was in to be next to the boy who was presumably Stephen Jenkins. She placed her hand on his shoulder and gently encouraged him saying, "You've read this before, you can do this. Don't be afraid."

Tentatively, the boy answered, "1867?"

"Well done," said the teacher.

"Did you see that?" I whispered to Finn.

"See what?"

"That boy got the right answer, and I think that woman helped him do it," I waited until the woman was facing away from us. With my loudest possible whisper, I said, "Eve... Eve. Don't worry and don't give up. You can do it and we're going to help you."

Maybe just my imagination, but Eve's eyes brightened before she buried her head in her folded arms.

"Get away from my classroom, now!" The only ones affected by the ghost woman's angry rebuke was us, the class sat as though we hadn't been there. I'd never seen a woman charge the way she did. My first reaction was to run, apparently so was Finn's because he took off before I could. We charged down the hallway into what appeared to be the main entry of the school. Two men, one in a white-sleeved red jacket, the other in a white-sleeved blue jacket, all four sleeves plastered with the activities each had been engaged in, turned to us then back to each other.

"You did not win the game in '56," snapped the blue jacket man.

"I'm about to prove it to you," red jacket man said, pointing as he walked to a case on the sidewall. "Look right there, back row… no, not that one, the round one with the wooden base. See. We won the championship game in '56."

Blue jacket stared quietly at the trophy for a long while. "You may have won, but you didn't even get off the bench in that game. I scored four touchdowns. The way I remember it you guys cheated a win on a technicality and a paid referee."

"You're so full of it. I was the starting quarterback and linebacker. Both ways, offense and defense. I was the best there was and the way I remember it you threw four interceptions, three of which I caught," red jacket shot back.

Blue jacket pretended to throw a pigskin. "You wouldn't have caught any of my passes. From what I remember you can't even jump over a quarter lying flat on its side, let alone one of my passes. Thirty-eight touchdowns my senior year. I guarantee you didn't even intercept one."

"Not even one? Try a dozen."

"You can't even count that high."

"Watch this. Is this only jumping over a quarter," red said as he leapt and slapped a point above him on the wall.

"That'd only be impressive if you were still hauling that fat butt of yours around. Watch this," blue said, not getting any higher than red. The men continued jumping at the wall as kids poured into the hallway. I was so wrapped up in their little contest that I'd missed the bell. In no time, kids with jackets and backpacks streamed out the front door. Buried in a tide of ten year olds, her head hung low, Eve rode the current to the school doors. I couldn't let her leave like that but I knew I couldn't get to her. I focused on her, and her chord returned. As soon as she was outside, I went to her. She stood on the sidewalk looking like she was ten going on forty. I touched her shoulder. She seemed to look toward me but said nothing.

"You're not alone. I'm going to help you," I said.

"We're going to help you." Finn was by my side. "We're going to help you."

Off to the rodeo

It never failed. Every time I went driving with Carl, and especially when we drove near Eve's house, I always felt the longing to have that experience with my little brother. Not the embarrassing *hope we aren't seen or considered to be stalking*, but the excitement of pursuing the fairer gender together. Sure he would have been ten years younger than me, seven years old or so, but I think I would have done much better with Finn at my side than Carl. If nothing else, I would have got the *you're such a nice guy to spend time with your little brother like that.* And now, in a very weird set of circumstances, my dead brother was my wingman to visit the girl of my dreams, who was now ten and at the moment far too young for me to date. Strange as this was, it filled that void.

"We're the first ones here. She doesn't look like she's having a nightmare," he said as we arrived in the room. The day had passed quickly. It felt weird to keep following Eve, so after school Finn took me to what I somehow knew was Niagara Falls. Rather than sightsee, we walked in the river to the edge of the cliff. Jumping off and screaming with my little brother, over and over again, was more fun than I could have imagined it to be.

Observing Eve's peaceful face, I wondered if I was in my own past or in some sort of alternate universe. Maybe the reason I was sent back in time was to get us together, or maybe it would prevent my own death, however it was that death overcame me.

"Taven, you've got that weird look on your face again," Finn said.

"I was just trying to figure something out," I said, hoping he wouldn't press me on it. Maybe I just needed to stop thinking about it.

"So we're going in the dream again, right?"

"That's the plan. We set things up so whatever it is she experiences tonight is not a nightmare. If we get in first, the dream junkies should have to play by our rules. We're going to make this as positive as we can, then build Eve up."

"This isn't going to work out like Janice, right?" Finn asked.

My voice came out more confident than I felt. "Eve will be fine. She's not Janice and we're not Janice's dad."

"Sorry. I just needed to hear you say it. Finn moved to the head of the bed. "So, where is this dream going to be set?"

"I know just the place," I said as I placed my hands on her head.

I imagined a space where great grey mountains sat on the straight horizon line, dividing the azure firmament from the rolling plains. An old fashioned fence made up of worn wooden posts about my height, connected by three rows of barbed wire, encircled a broad area, which would serve as the stage for the dream. Within the grounds were horse stables, pristine, as if they'd come from a little girl's play set, although large enough to house the real things. I peppered the plains surrounding the enclosure with Birch, Fir, Maple, Ash, Walnut, Juniper, Larch, Spruce and Pine trees, all in their native splendor, inviting and life giving, never so dense so as to cut off the light. To the north of the enclosure, I drew a lazy stream that meandered from east to west, pooling here and there in welcoming springs. Mallards, Canadian geese, greater prairie chickens, peregrine falcons, blue jays and great horned owls, nested in the pleasantly populated forest. And last but not least I imagined horses, and in particular, a mare with a chestnut sheen, black mane, powerful neck and majestic standing.

Somehow I knew, not remembered, that Eve was a cowboy at heart. Some of her most fond memories, which she must have expressed to me at some point, were those she had of the ranch where she spent her summers. She absolutely loved the horses and the land.

Finn and I stood in the middle of the enclosure, the horse stables situated at the west end. "Now this is a lot better than that rotten old house," said Finn as the paradise of my imagination rolled out before us.

The product was in fact better than imagination. The oxygen produced by the trees was sweet and pure and seemed to be in higher concentration than average air, because it enlivened the senses and connected us with the living world around us.

Having taken a particularly satisfying breath, I turned to my brother. "Breathing never felt so good... Umm... So I like your tights, but you kind of look out of place."

"I had no idea where you were taking me so I went with the standard hero outfit. But thanks for the reminder, sometimes I lose track of what I'm wearing," he said now in dark blue straight-cut blue jeans, plaid shirt and a great big white cowboy hat. Not wanting to be outdone, I imagined a matching outfit for myself, only with a striped shirt rather than a plaid one.

"Let's go find Eve," I said.

"Yee haw!" Finn ran across the field and towards the largest stable, looking so much like the two-year old little boy he was in life, not that he ran like he was about to topple over, but when he ran, he exuded joy: unfettered and irresistible happiness. Throwing my hands into the air, I opened my mouth to take in as much of the delicious air as I could as I ran along beside him.

Reaching the stable doors of the main building, I pushed them open while Finn ran to the next building over. I entered the long broad alley, bordered by eight stalls on each side, filled with unspoiled straw. And there she was. At the far end on the barn, she sat alone on a stool, dressed in her nightgown, and motionless.

"Eve, come on over. Let's go for a ride," I called.

She shook her head, refusing to look at me.

Conjuring up a small pink cowboy hat, I approached her as I would someone who was about to jump off of a bridge, holding up the hat as a token of peace. I said, "I know you love to ride horses, let me bring one to you."

"No," she screamed. "Stay away. Leave me alone. I don't want to be here. I don't want to do this anymore. Leave me alone."

"Don't you like horses?" I asked still edging towards her.

"No," she cried. "Get away. Stop. I don't want you to hurt me."

"Don't you remember me? I helped you last night. Do you remember?" She looked at me as though I was some vague recollection but uncertain enough not to be trusted.

"If you come, they're going to hurt me," she said.

"No they won't. This is a beautiful place made specifically for you. Don't you like horses?" I asked.

"Not ones like that."

"Like wh…" I began, until I was interrupted by a crash at the stall next to Eve. The stall's iron gate shot over her head. I sprinted toward her, too far to protect her, but close enough to see the mutated mare, its mouth filled with jagged teeth, which prevented it from fully closing, its hair long and shaggy, and its eyes, including its pupils, were white. It pawed the ground as though it was about to charge her.

The moment I saw the abomination, the hallway seemed to lengthen beyond any distance I could cover in order to rescue her. What I wouldn't have given for another remote control, but in a moment roller skates were on my feet and I was gaining on the retreating back end of the barn.

Still too far to prevent it from causing harm, the horse turned away from Eve and positioned its legs as though it would kick her with its hind legs.

"Run," I shouted as its powerful legs began to recoil.

Finn, out of nowhere, with hat in hand, flew from the stall on the other side of the barn and onto the back of the now bucking bronco, yanking on its mane, driving his spurs into its sides, forcing it from Eve at the last possible moment.

"Yee haw!" he yelled again, one hand gripped in the tangled mane, the other hand flailing behind him, as the horse circled, kicking wildly in attempt to unseat my brother. "Get us outside, Taven."

There not being time to get them out a door, I unimagined the building and in a flash we were all outside in the vast gated field. Eve still sat on a three cornered stool, some distance from the impromptu rodeo, which was between her and I.

She was now at least half a football field away. I embraced the idea of a frog-like hop and leapt, wind lashing my face, the air-cooling as I gained altitude. I soon found myself directly over my brother and the crazed horse, sailing gracefully towards her until I jerked like a dog that had unexpectedly come to the end of its leash. I crashed to the earth, within stomping distance of the mutated equine. Barbed wire crept further around my waste. Already looped two times, the sharp edges tore my shirt and gouged my skin. A wooden post, less than a stone's throw away, wielded the barbed wire, a total of six strands, like bull whips. It cracked the barbed whips at an oblivious Finn.

"Watch out!" I yelled.

He responded by looking in my direction, which shift in attention caused him to lose his balance. He was sent flying into the air, landing next to the raging horse but a little out of the range of the barbed wire beast. The cord, now coiled around me almost three times, tightened around my torso.

An unnatural glowering storm cloud swept across the blue sky, jolting thunder bolts directly beneath it. It's trajectory was straight to Eve.

In spite of the growing pain, all I could think of was helping her, and in that moment of desperation, I remembered that in order to help her, I needed to help her help herself. I rejected the idea of the suit of armor that flashed into mind. "Eve! We need your help. You can help us. You can do it."

"No, I can't," she screamed back.

"It's your dream. You can do it. You can help us. I know you can."

"I can't. I can't. I can't."

The cords around my torso now were so tight that I could no longer speak. I saw Finn was now dressed as a rodeo clown, dancing playfully in front of the horse, leading it away from Eve. The cloud was now nearly directly over top of her. Rescuing her wasn't the solution to the problem, but it was a stopgap measure that could buy us enough time to figure out how to help her help herself. Accepting the idea, I was now clothed in a suit of armor, which as it formed itself around my body, snapped my barbed wire bonds. "Finn, the cloud!"

As I ran at the wooden post, I saw Finn turn his attention to the cloud and waive at it so as to distract it from Eve. I drew the broadsword that had materialized at my side. The strands of barbed wire flailed at me without effect other than the sound of metal against metal. One by one, I severed the strands until at last I arrived at the wooden post, which without hesitation, I sliced in two.

"Take this," I shouted as I tossed a strand of the barbed wire to Finn, which easily bridged the great distance between us.

My brother snagged the cord out of mid-air and dodged the stampeding horse as though he had known its course in advance. He positioned himself behind it and slipped the loop he had formed in the barbed wire while dodging the horse around its hind leg.

The storm cloud had drifted nearly to him, lightning bolts crashing into the ground, sending shards of earth into the air. As though the cord was a lasso, Finn spun the end not attached to the horse over his head.

"Let's rope us some cloud," he shouted as he released the makeshift rope. The loop at the end of the wire extended as it approached the cloud until it was easily large enough to fit over it. Once around the cloud, it responded to Finn's tug and tightened around the cloud stopping at its tangible core. The bolts of lightning had not stopped and no sooner had Finn completed the electric circuit between the horse and the cloud than a jolt of electricity streamed down the cord frying the horse, annihilating the cloud and sending Finn, who at that point had his hands on the barbed wire, flying backwards.

Eve's "No," hung in the air with my cry of "Finn!"

As soon as I imagined the brown chestnut mare, it was beneath me. I rode to Finn's side, slid off the horse, removed my helmet and gauntlet and knelt next to him. My baby brother was motionless for the second time in the past twenty-four hours and it was my fault. I put my hand on his shoulder and lightly shook him. "Are you alright?"

Finn opened his eyes and lifted his cut and charred hands to me. "Have you got a Band-Aid? I feel like I've got a really bad paper cut or something."

Before I could emit anything more than an uncomfortable groan, Eve appeared at my side, slightly out of breath, with a small bottle between her hands. "Here. Use this. It will help you feel better." She uncorked the top and motioned for Finn to hold out his hands.

Finn hesitated. "What is that?"

"It's special medicine. My dad says my great grandma used to have a special medicine that fixed almost anything. When I saw you get shocked, I thought about what I could do and the medicine was in my hands."

Finn held out his hands. Eve tilted the bottle. The instant the liquid touched his flesh, it was back to normal. "Ah, that feels so much better. Thanks!"

Eve smiled freely. I asked her, "Are you not scared any more?"

"I feel afraid, but when I saw him get hurt, I knew I had to do something. So I did."

"Thanks little girl. I really appreciate it." Finn held out his hand for a high-five, and having received it, turned to me and said, "I'm going to take a look around to make sure everything's okay."

"Sounds good. I'll stay here with Eve." I couldn't even say her name anymore without the image of how I remembered her coming to mind. I took a deep breath. This had to be her. "Do you remember me?"

"You seem familiar." She paused for a moment then continued, "I know you. You're the guy that keeps getting beat up in all my dreams."

Not quite what I was hoping for, but I wasn't sure I could have what I hoped for anyway. I was dead and she was only ten years old. "We're here to help you. To rescue you from..."

But Eve was no longer looking at me. Her gaze was fixed behind me. I turned to see Fiona, dressed in a long black cloak. In the background, I saw Finn sprawled out on the ground, with Ben and Dan standing over him.

Before I could open my mouth, Eve screamed, "Leave him alone!"

Fiona walked within a few paces of me. "Did you miss me?"

"What did you do to him?" I asked.

"Worried about your little brother, Taven? You should be more worried about yourself," she said, striking me with such force I was driven into the ground, my shoulder acting like a plow.

All I could see was earth, I couldn't move. Everything smelt of dirt. There was no air. I was bound, crushed and panicking. I barely felt the hands around my ankle but I heard the muffled voice, "Don't worry. I'll get you out of there." They were coming from Eve.

I heard a cry and then a man's response, "What are you going to do about it? What can you do about it? You are useless and you are helpless..."

At that moment a lit stick of dynamite came to mind. I hesitated briefly, unsure whether I'd be blown to bits, but trusting the impression I laid hold on it. I couldn't see the explosive, but I could hear the hiss of the fire as it moved along the wick.

"Watch out," I heard a gruff voice yell as the ground around me shot up, firework-like, into the air. I rose out of the earth unharmed, in what must have been an impressive scene. Fiona was sprawled out on the ground. Pulled along by her hair, Dan led Eve away from me. My stomach dropped when I saw the newly formed cliff on the edge of the paradise I'd created. My horror was accentuated by the young girls screams of terror.

My horse was next to me. I leapt on it and galloped at the pair, a jousting stick in hand. Before reaching Dan, I was intercepted by Ben, who charged at me on all fours like a beast, using his arms to yank himself forward and his legs to leap and continue the momentum. I turned at the last moment and speared him in the chest with my weapon sending him to the ground.

Without warning I was thrown from my horse. I looked back and saw it was buried knee high in the soil. It threw its head, struggling to free itself. Fiona calmly walked towards me. Despite being some distance from me, I heard her whisper. "What are you going to do?"

"I'm going to stop you," I yelled leaving my horse.

"It's not me you need to worry about," she said, motioning towards the cliff.

Dan held Eve, by her ankle, over the edge of the cliff. She thrashed but Dan was unmoved by her effort.

"Don't worry, Eve, I'll save you!" But I didn't know how.

"Sure you will." Dan said, in a normal voice that echoed across the clearing, as he released his grip.

Eve screamed, I shouted and all was lost… I thought.

"I got one!" Finn, now fully dressed in fishing gear, sat on the edge of the cliff some distance from Dan with a long pole in hand. He quickly reeled the line in. Up came Eve, with a life preserver around her waist. Finn steadied her then placed her back on the ground. "There you go."

A crease along the edge of the cliff appeared, the tremble in the earth knocking Finn and Eve down.

"Good bye!" shouted a gruff voice as the chunk of earth fell over the edge and everything went dark as I was sucked out of the dream.

I arrived in the bedroom, where an alarm rang in the background. To my relief, Finn stood unharmed. Eve stirred in her bed. Fiona stood apart from Ben and Dan.

"If you don't stop us," said Fiona, "It's only a matter of time before we destroy her."

Ben looked like the only thing keeping him from me was an invisible chain around his neck. Dan smirked, probably gloating over the fact he'd had the last laugh. Fiona looked directly at Finn, then walked to and touched Ben and Dan, all three of them disappearing from the room, leaving only Fiona's, "See you tomorrow," hanging in the air.

"Can someone shut that alarm off?" I said. As though she'd heard me, Eve lifted her arm and blindly felt for the snooze button. "Are we just making things worse? Are we doing the same things to Eve, as Janice's father did to her?"

"Taven, you were right. This is not the same and I'm not so sure we failed."

"What do you mean?"

"Let's get out of here first. Eve's about to wake up and I think if nothing else, she deserves privacy." Finn touched my arm. In an instant we were back in the clearing. The joggers and early morning dog walkers were out. In an instant they were gone, and we were in the hazy other world. "Watch this!"

Finn placed his finger on my forehead. I was with he and Eve on the edge of the cliff from Eve's dream. We weren't close enough to see over the edge. The ground shook and we all fell to the ground. We tilted. Far beneath us was a dry riverbed. I started to slide, Eve was screaming. I couldn't see Finn. I fell off the edge. Eve lost her grip and plummeted. Wafts of strands of pink were all around me, increasing in density until they slowed and ultimately stopped my descent. Eve ended up near me.

"It's cotton candy. Try it. It's the real thing," said Finn, who was next to Eve and I.

I grabbed a strand and put it to my mouth. "Bubble gum," I said, in unison with Eve.

"Best dream ever!" she yelled. An alarm sounded vaguely overhead. "Time to get up already?"

The scene in front of me transitioned back to the present.

I held my hand up and received a high-five from my brother. "Finn, that was awesome. You are the best."

"See, I told you you were right. I think she's fine. I'm not even sure she would need us anymore against Ben and Dan," he said.

"And Fiona," I added.

"Mostly Ben and Dan, Taven."

"You mean she still needs our help because of Fiona?" I asked.

"No, that's not what I mean." Finn did not look like he was joking. "She is not who she seems to be."

I remembered Fiona touching his arm. "Whatever she told you, you can't believe a word of it."

"But…"

"Not a word of it. She is evil. She was using me to destroy Eve. How is that not evil? Anybody who would use a person the way she used me to get what she wanted is evil."

"Are you sure about that reasoning?" he asked.

"Pretty sure. She was everything she warned me that you and the family were. She was using you as a cover for who she really was and what she was going to do. And did you see her hit me? I thought I was going to suffocate down there."

"That was nothing more than a good tackle. This is a game for her. A high stakes game, but a game. She's playing it because she has to, and if she doesn't play it well, she's… she's…"

"Falling for the devil are you, Finn?" It was what I wanted to ask, but not how I would have said it. But it wasn't me. It was Ben.

"Oh no, you shouldn't fall for me. All you'll get is pain." Before I could think, Ben had pinned me to the ground. He turned my head so I could watch. I couldn't do anything other than experience what was happening. Fiona was facing Finn.

"So what if I am?" Finn said. "She isn't what you think she is."

"Shut your mouth," Fiona cried. "Stop standing there and grab him."

Dan seemed surprised at Fiona's command. He tackled Finn to the ground. Finn didn't even seem to resist. He looked to her. "Don't worry. I know who you are."

"And because of you your brother is about to find out first hand," she said. Fiona pulled a glowing whip from the air and slung it at Finn, striking both he and Dan. Both lay motionless. She turned toward me. The strand flew at me. As the world went dark, I heard a woman's voice say, "Don't give up. No matter what."

Abducted

Rhythmic, unending. Water dropping into water echoed in my ears. Drip. Drip. Drip. *Is this the extent of my experience?* Drip. Drip. Drip. *My existence?* Drip. Drip. Drip. *But what am I? I can think. I can hear water. I am near water. I must be a pebble in a streambed? No, I am more than rock.* Drip. *How do I know what water is?*

Images danced just outside of my perception, like they were waiting on the other side of a frosted piece of glass. At first I didn't care much about them, but there I somehow knew they were important. My desire to comprehend grew until I was able to focus on the glass. Pain returned, but it's as though the glass cracked in response to my effort. The agony increased but the need to see what was on the other side strengthened me. The glass cleared. I saw myself. *Now I'm with another man on the edge of the water. He's throwing something. Why do I feel so strongly for him? My feelings for him are not bitter but something about him is. Is there something wrong? Wait, I remember.*

"Finn? Are you here too?" Memory shattered the mental prison.

I opened my eyes, but saw nothing. I tried to stand but was trapped. I drew a picture of the clearing in my mind, but rather than movement, it was as though acid was poured on my brain causing extreme suffering and corroding the picture from my mind. When the pain eased to the point that I could again take in information through my senses, the sound of the drip had ceased or was now overshadowed by the growing sound of raging fire, which grew in intensity until I expected I would be engulfed in flames. Instead the fire spoke as a voice, whether audibly or in my mind, I could not tell.

"Give them to me."

I had no idea who the voice was talking about, but even if I did I know I wasn't going to comply. "No."

No sooner had I answered, than I saw what looked like a roll of film in my mind. On each square was a face. They began to scroll before me. It was all a blur until I saw Chief, then uncle Bennett, my father, my mother, my sister and Finn. "No!"

"Give them to me." A grey light illuminated the room. The roof of the cavern, which had recently pressed down on me, was now above me. I was alone in the room, at least there was no one I could see. "Taven. Why do you waste your time fighting a battle that will surely be lost? The weakest of my servants have overpowered you and now, against your will and in accordance with mine, you are here with me, in my power."

I opened my mouth to interrupt and voice my disapproval, but pain accompanied my attempt.

"You see. I have all power here and you will only act as permitted by me." I attempted to stand, but it felt as though a boot was pressed against my neck. "Stubborn and strong. You will be an excellent asset to my army. Give them to me."

It seemed as though a hand had reached into my mind and was attempting to pull the list from me. I concentrated on the list. I was not going to let it go without a fight. "You cannot have it. You'll have to destroy me first."

"So be it." The room went silent. I sat up. Across the room from me, the rocks in the wall of the cave began to stir. I backed away just as they spilled onto the ground in front of me, far too close for comfort. Invisible hands molded the clay. Four cylindrical pieces were formed along with a round one. They were placed together. The thing took the shape of a faceless humanoid.

Before I could raise my hands, the creature brandished a red whip, which wrapped around my neck and pulled me to the ground. I felt physical pain and disappointment, failure, hopelessness. I felt the chord release from my neck. "Give them to me, and it will all be over."

"Never." Intending to charge at and ultimately overpower the being I attempted to stand, but before I'd gotten to my knees, the whip cracked across my chest, throwing me to my back. I heard the whip snap across my chest again and saw my parents, my beloved parents, buried to the neck in what looked like cement, surrounded by vultures. They loomed in too close, threatening to pull the flesh off their living faces. "No!"

"You will give them to me eventually. It is only a matter of time. None can resist my power."

"You can, Taven." A woman's voice, quiet and gentle momentarily dispersed the pain.

"How?" I asked as the pain erased any echo the voice could have left.

"You ask me how?" This was not the woman's voice. I was thrown to my face. Finn was in my mind, hands and feet tied between two horses, each facing an opposite direction. Faceless demons stood at the rear of each horse.

I attempted to stand but was too weak. The faceless monster stood over me. It raised its arm, I closed my eyes. The little girl Eve stood before me. "I hate you. You've ruined my life.

Everything's gone wrong because of you. I wish I was dead and I wish you were too. It was then I realized we were on a building, overlooking downtown. Before I could stop her, Eve jumped. Her scream echoed in my ears as I stood watching her. But it wasn't her. It was all in my mind. I knew it was because I knew. I knew that was not her. I opened my eyes to see the pathetic life form and hear the crashing fire. With renewed strength, I spoke a single word, "Liar."

The thing raised its arm to strike me but before it could I sprung to my feet and grabbed both its wrists. I was surprised by its strength, it seemed as though I was pushing against a trash compactor. I was thrown to the ground. Its boot was at my throat. I saw myself. I stood alone in the midst of a barren waste. My head hung low. I could not die and was doomed to live in oblivion.

"Bring me someone else," the fiery voice began, dispelling the vision, "and I'll let you keep your family for now."

A woman's face came into view. I had never seen her before, but no sooner had she come into my mind than I knew everything about her, or so it seemed. Her name was Daniela. She was the matriarch of a large family and had recently died.

"Bring her to me and you may keep your family for now. Or, if you prefer, we can continue." The being wrapped the whip around my neck. After the initial shock of the sensation of strangulation, memory and fear flooded my being: memory of loss

278

- it was like Finn died again and again and the feeling of the moment remained, and fear over all that could have happened and would happen as a result of my weakness. It felt like I was suffocating. The desire to stop the suffering grew and as it grew, the immorality of subjecting another soul to this suffering so that I could escape it seemed more and more acceptable.

My submission to the fiery voice had been formulated and was about to be spoken, when the woman's voice returned. "Taven, don't give in. I need you. Please, don't give in. You can do it. Hold on."

"Who are you?" I asked aloud.

The sound of fire grew louder. But it was drowned out, at least for me, by the quiet and still whisper, "Eve."

Unexpected help

I don't even know how Eve had asked for my help, but she did. And her plea for help was enough to give me the strength to endure imagination that was as acute as experience, seeing my loved ones and myself subject to devilish torment and destruction more times than I cared to count. After what seemed like an eternity, the fiery voice lost patience. The grey light was extinguished. And there was silence broken only by the dripping of the water. In the dark, in the monotony of the experience, I found it increasingly difficult to maintain hold of myself. I was alone and my mind had been so seared by the experience that I could no longer summon positive experience. It was like I was clinging to the short-term memory of the people I loved, because if I stopped running their names through my mind, I was going to forget them.

It wasn't long before that was what happened and all that was left was the idea of Eve's voice coming to me. And it was slipping between my fingers. If I lost it, I felt as though I'd lose myself. My grip loosened further and it was as though I was now looking into the abyss into which I was going to fall.

But light burst into the room. I opened my eyes. It was not the grey light, but a light like the first rising of the sun. A shadowy figure stood before me. "Finn? How did you find me?"

"I just followed the smell."

"Stop fooling around. We need to get him out of here." The voice was familiar. My great great grandfather, Chief slipped in through the newly formed hole in the wall. "Taven, my boy. You had us worried. We were thrown a bit of a curveball we didn't expect. But we're here now so don't you worry."

"Where am I?" I asked as a bearded face poked through the entry. "Uncle Bennett?"

"Kane's lair," he said. Having stepped through the hole, he walked up to me and picked me off the ground and into his arms. "This is not what we intended. We were out hunting gophers and we ended up in the snake's den."

"What do you mean?" I asked.

Finn looked to the ground and Uncle Bennett looked at Chief. Chief took a step towards me and put a hand on my shoulder. "We used you..."

"Fiona was right?" I asked. "She told me all along you were using me."

"It's not like that Taven," said Uncle Bennett, "but we don't have a lot of time to explain. We need to get out of here before we're found out."

"I'm not leaving." I said.

"What? You have to come. I can't leave you here..." Finn began.

I turned to Finn. "I don't want you to leave me here. Now it's my turn to use you. Not to use you, but I need your help. I can't believe something this evil is more powerful than good. I just don't know how to fight it. Like I didn't in the dreams. I need you to tell me what I need to know to fight it. And now is the time. Whatever this thing is, I'm not going to let it do this to anyone else without a fight."

I could tell by the look on Finn's face he didn't know how to answer that question.

"We are out of our league here," said Chief. "We knew if we left you on your own you would run into the dream junkies. It was only a matter of time before they infiltrated our family using the same pattern. They find someone who has recently passed over to this side and use them for their family connections. Once they've obtained a connection they feast on the weak, or rather, they overwhelm the weak and as they do the strong are weakened. We thought it was best if it was you they influenced and that's why I told the family not to communicate with you, not to give you too much information because if you fell, I didn't want it used against us. But I never thought you would have taken them into dreams. At least the dead can see and combat these monsters. But the living, little Eve, has no defense…"

"Yes, she does," said Finn. "She has family here and there that is there for her. And that counts for something. Us being involved counts for something and she is stronger because of it. This wasn't where we wanted to be, but because we're here, we've learned we can make a real difference…"

"Remember Janice. Remember how her father tried to help her and only led her down a path of self-veneration and self-loathing. It was because he tried to help. It was because he went into the dreams and now we've done the same to Eve…" said Chief.

Uncle Bennett interrupted. "I don't believe that. I know you are the leader of our family but I have never believed that and I am ashamed it took all this to give me the courage to speak up. I have to believe Janice always had a choice. The fact she latched onto self-veneration was a choice she would have made once presented with the option. Her father may be guilty of presenting the option, but Janice is the one who made the choice."

Uncle Bennett turned to me and placed a hand on my shoulder. Strength flowed into me from the point of contact. "I think you're right. We're not here by coincidence." Uncle Bennett motioned with a tilt of his head for Finn to speak.

"Someone told me how to find you..." Finn paused. "After you disappeared, Fiona told me how to find you and she told me how to escape."

"You trusted her? Don't you think this could all be a trap?" I asked. "She used me to get into Eve's dream. Now she's used me to get you all trapped here."

"Taven, she isn't what you think. She lived once like us. She died once like us. She loves her family like us. She's doing the best she can with her circumstances. She saw a strength in you and she decided to take a risk. She told me she never intended to do as Kane told her but she went along acting, waiting for her moment to break free. When she met you, and saw the strength of your will, she hoped you would be the one to rescue her."

"Rescue her?" I said. "You are asking me to rescue the person who has been leading the charge to destroy me, my family, Eve and everyone else who's important to me?"

"She had no choice... she told you not to believe her. I saw the same thing you did. She told me." Finn put his hand on my forehead. The vision of the little girl flashed into memory. "It was her who spoke to you when you were being tortured. I know she said she was Eve but she only did that because I told her you wouldn't believe her."

"How long have you been talking to her like this? Why didn't you tell me?" I asked.

"I tried to but you wouldn't listen. After you disappeared she sent Ben and Dan away so she could 'deal' with me herself. They were very reluctant to leave. It wasn't until she threatened to use the whip on them that they finally left. Once they were gone, she charged at me as though she would strike me then grabbed my wrist and... kissed me." If there was blood in my brother's face, his cheeks would have flushed. "She thanked me for believing her, she told me she could tell by the way I looked at her. I asked you where you went and that's when she told me. She knew you had met Elmer and hoped you had learned something from him. He is one of the few that escaped where we are. He did it with force and the strength of his will. The devils couldn't stop him. She knew you were strong enough to take the suffering and once you did, you would know what Elmer knew and be able to escape."

"Then why are you here?" I asked.

Uncle Bennett spoke. "Because we knew you wouldn't try to escape once you got in here. We knew you'd try to finish this and we didn't want you to be on your own."

"And how did you know that?"

"Let's just say, my boy, my great boy, some things don't change," said Chief.

All three of them stood looking at me and I had no idea what the next step was. "Elmer escaped from here? I would have figured he was a devil."

"Nope," said Finn. "Not a devil but a nasty stubborn guy."

"Maybe that's why he escaped," said Bennett.

"Because he's nasty?" asked Finn.

"No, because he's stubborn. Because he didn't give in." Chief turned to me. "And neither did you."

In a few minutes I went from the edge of painful oblivion to a clear perception of and awakening of my potential. A thought pressed itself on me. "What's stopping us from doing with our minds what we're able to do in the dreams?"

It was clear Uncle Bennett and Chief had no idea what I was talking about. Finn said, "You mean lay hold on the bursts of inspiration to give us the tools we need to succeed?"

"Exactly. And we know how to defend ourselves. If Elmer was strong enough to break out and we are strong enough to resist Elmer's strength, then we are strong enough to find this... this... what did you say his name is?"

"Kane," said Uncle Bennett. "He is the keeper of the thirteen citadels of Sheol."

An idea of a door pressed itself on my mind. "Then let's go meet Kane." I walked past my three rescuers and concentrated on the idea. The faint outline of a door appeared in the wall opposite the hole. "Are you guys coming?"

"Wait. What's your plan?" asked Chief.

"Don't have one and we're not going to need one," I answered.

Uncle Bennett stepped in front of me. "Slow down. Let's figure this out."

"The plan is simple. Trust that good is stronger than bad and trust your instincts. When the ideas come, hold to them. Are you coming?" It sounded crazy coming out of my mouth, but I knew it was right.

Finn walked to the outline in the wall. A sledgehammer was in his hand. "I'm with you," he said as he slammed the wall. The rocks slipped backward in response to his blow.

A headlamp was strapped to Chief's forehead. He turned it on, lighting the room as though it was midday. "A place like this needs a little light."

Uncle Bennett turned to me. "I'm with you, Taven." He lowered his shoulder and crashed through the wall.

Finn, Chief and I followed Bennett out of the room and into a spacious cave. Winged humanoid creatures flew near the top of the space, far above our heads. Chief dimmed his light. "I don't think we want those things spotting us."

"I think we do." I reached over and switched the light on full. The humanoids screeched like crows with a megaphone and began circling down at us. The rubble from the makeshift door was drawn back into the wall. It was sealed as though we'd never broken through. There was no going back.

One of the creatures dove at us. Its head split in two from the crown of its head to the base of its neck revealing rows of shark-like teeth. I could see no eyes and no ears. Rather than fingers, sharp spikes lined the palms of its hands and jutted out of the nubs of its ankles. Its skin looked as though it was made of latex. My mind was blank as it careened toward me. I ran but it adjusted to catch me and pointed its claws at me. I prepared myself for contact still nothing in mind.

There was a blast that echoed through the space. I leapt out of the way as the lifeless creature fell to the ground and disintegrated on contact. "Whatever those things are, this seems to work on them." Chief patted the oversized rifle in his hands.

Dozens of the humanoids now dove from the ceiling. Uncle Bennett tossed a gigantic net, capturing three of the things and pinning them to the wall far from us. Finn held out a rod as four streamed at him. When they were close enough, a visible charge of electricity grounded all four of them. Chief discharged his rifle dropping one after another, requiring the rest of us to dodge the bodies falling from the sky. I was feeling pretty useless. Here I was, taking the lead on this impromptu mission, and I was doing nothing more than dodging lifeless bodies. And then it got worse.

One of the beasts made it through and hooked its claws into my arms and legs and swooped up toward the roof. The points of contact felt like the whip, only they did not prevent my ability to think. In the midst of the pain, I remembered Elmer, the man who played games, the man who escaped.

I focused on the points of contact and drove the negative energy out of me. It must have entered the humanoid because it cried out in pain and attempted to detach itself from me but before it could it burst into a cloud of blackened ashes. From twenty stories above my family I began to fall. The blade of a food processor came into mind. I focused on it and attached to my ankles were blades that spread out to the sides of the cavern. A large umbrella was instantly in my right hand. I shook off the creature that had attached itself to my left arm and started to spin as I slowly descended from the top of the cave. As I descended, the blades continued to extend. The remaining humanoids were diced as I descended, each bursting into the same darkened cloud. With the last of them being dismantled, the umbrella and blades vanished and I dropped to the ground from about three times my height.

Finn, Uncle Bennett and Chief were covered in a what looked like dirty snow. "Thanks for that," said Chief.

"At least we know the premise of Taven's plan seems to be accurate," said Uncle Bennett.

"Kind of tastes like chalk," said Finn as he licked his finger.

Our success was short-lived. The walls of the cavern extended out further leaving us in the middle of the room. Doors now lined the walls, stacked one on top of another from the bottom to near the top of the ceiling.

What began as a crackle, grew into the sound of a roaring fire. From the noise of the bonfire sprang words. "There are cockroaches in my house. Destroy them."

A single door opened. A old-looking man dressed in what appeared to be a worn burlap sack slowly made his way toward us. Hunched over, he walked as though he needed a cane, but did not have one. The texture of his muscles was visible through his skin and his face was tired. I pitied him until he looked at me with eyes that were hungry and hollow. He stopped and let out a scream that was angry, hungry and tortured. Finn, Chief, uncle Bennett and I pressed closer together. The man broke out into a full out sprint and leapt, covering the distance that separated us from him. Uncle Bennett stepped up and with a bat in hand connected with the man sending him lifelessly twisting toward the back wall. The man slammed into one of the doors and fell to the ground.

The door he struck began to open. A woman, dressed like the man, but who seemed as though she could be an attractive woman were it not for her unkempt hair and her air of savagery, dropped from the portal to the ground. The man rose from the ground and approached as he had the first time. She walked more briskly and stopped ahead of the man. She waited for him to arrive, never taking her eyes off of us. Like the first time, both howled, and then charged at us. A gigantic slingshot appeared in front of Finn, which caught the woman then flung her against the wall hitting another door. Uncle Bennett struck the man again, sending him skidding across the ground. The man got back up and walked away from us to the wall. Once he arrived at the wall, he knocked on one of the doors.

The door the woman hit opened to reveal a bald obese man, similarly dressed. The knocked on door opened to reveal a rail thin woman with hair that was chopped just above her shoulders. Same clothes. Like the others, each walked to a spot the same distance from us and waited for the others. All four sprung at us. Chief fired his rifle at all four of them, one after the other, sending them to the ground. A rope in mind, I ran to them, intending to tie them up and prevent them from knocking on any other doors. As I swung the rope around the large man, he reached for me. The same electricity, only more like the shock I felt with Fiona coursed through the point of contact, causing me to jump back. The large man stood and turned away. I looped the rope and tossed it over him, catching him around the chest. I pulled hard but rather than pull him over, he caught the rope and twisted quickly pulling me off balance and sending me to the floor. He ran to the wall and knocked. Hoping Finn, uncle Bennett and Chief had had more luck I looked only to find them likewise sprawled on the ground with their attackers making their way back to the walls.

Four more doors were knocked on. Four more doors opened. Different looking people, but the same results. The four of us gathered back in the middle of the floor as we watched the eight make there way to us. They leapt at us. Finn was in the cockpit of a wrecking ball machine. He pulled the lever and sent five of the people flying to the wall. A horse materialized under Chief and cowboy-like, I wasn't sure if Finn had filled him in on the dream and he wanted to show me up, he lassoed and hog-tied two more together. One of the two touched him, sending him stumbling back from them. The eighth made it to uncle Bennett and they were locked in a pushing contest, although my uncle howled in pain. With the oven mitts that had sprung to mind, I grabbed the thing and tossed him at the wall with so much force that all the doors rattled.

"Get over here, quickly," I yelled to Finn and Chief. As soon as they had arrived, the circular wall that had been in my mind built itself around and domed over the top of us. Muffled through the stones, the creaking of thousands of doors was around us. I knew we didn't have much time. "Uncle Bennett, why were you in so much pain?"

"When she grabbed me, it was like I was dying from cancer all over again, only this time it was my fault and…"

I stopped him. "This is the power Elmer used on us. It doesn't have to affect us… its just like the power of the whip."

"So we use Kane's power against him?" Finn asked.

"No, we won't. But we need him to come." Muted thuds and otherworldly shrieks interrupted us. I turned to Chief. "Can we carve him out of our family connections? Out of Fiona's?"

"I don't know if they're the same as us. I don't know if it is even possible to carve anyone out," he said.

"But you said you were going to carve us out," Finn said.

The sound outside was growing louder. The rocks separating us from them began to shift out of place. "The idea came to mind when I heard what Taven had done. I could see what needed to be done to carve someone out."

"Then tell me what to do," I said. "I'll do it. He'll come to me."

"I saw myself putting my hands on your shoulders. Once I did, I saw inside your mind. A long flowing banner, with the images of the family, hung there. I saw myself tear the fabric from your mind, leaving you alone." Chief paused. If I didn't know better I would have thought he was composing himself. "It is not easy being the leader of a people, Taven."

"I understand and I don't blame you." In my mind I saw the crowd of people part and Kane walk to us. "Good will come of this. I'm about to take down the wall. Don't believe what they tell you, the imaginations they put in your heart and mind. Hang on and don't fight back."

"I'm with you big brother," Finn replied.

I focused on the wall and in an instant it was gone. A wave of bodies surrounded us and crashed in on us. It was like I was being stung by an entire colony of bees only the venom was torment. But I knew I didn't have to give in. When I heard uncle Bennett moan, a vision of my sister being dragged by her hair began to materialize but I quickly shunned it.

I don't know how long we remained in the mangle of bodies but it stopped as abruptly as it started. The crowd stood and backed away from us, clearing a large enough path for a single person to come to us. Chief and uncle Bennett looked worn but determined. Finn had a gleam in his eye and a smirk on his lips.

The rumble of the fire erupted into words. "All kneel before Kane."

The instant I heard the voice, the mass of bodies, my companions and the dungeon we were in were replaced by gently rolling water out to the horizon. I could feel the grains of sand between my toes and the warmth of the sun on my face. The waves lapped the shore. Fiona stood next to me dressed in a floral print dress that danced in the wind behind her. A flower was in her hair. She motioned for me to come to her. The vision took my breath.

I wanted to be with her more than anything else at that moment. It only made sense that I would. She had helped me, in the beginning and now in the end. If it wasn't for her I'd still be in Kane's lair, not here with her. But as much as I knew or thought I knew I wanted her, I couldn't get the fact that she had kissed Finn and he had kissed her out of my mind. I reasoned that it couldn't be wrong if I wanted it so bad, could it?

I took a step toward Fiona but was stopped by the thought I would be betraying Eve if I went any further.

My choice was clear and simple. Stretch out my hand and get what I wanted now or wait and trust the voice within me. Whenever I thought of the inner voice, I seemed to understand this was only a dream, my family and I were Kane's prisoners. When I thought of Fiona, it didn't matter, whether I was a prisoner or not, as long as I had what I wanted, and I wanted her. But what was it I wanted. Beyond the desire for a beautiful woman, what was there?

"Taven, it's a trap," Fiona cried. Not the woman on the beach, but the same voice I'd heard before. "This is not me."

The Fiona in the vision lunged for me as I focused back on the dungeon.

Hundreds were bowed around Finn, Uncle Bennett, Chief and I. "Are you okay?" asked Finn.

"I'm fine."

I was interrupted by what sounded like a clap of thunder that matched the step of a man walking up the aisle towards us. Each footstep seemed to shake the room. A hulking man with an Adonis-like figure approached us. He wore sandals and a loincloth. A metallic miniature bundle of wheat hung around his neck and grey chains were draped over his shoulders and wrapped around his wrists.

"Kneel before me," cried Kane. He didn't wait for a response, but brandishing the same whip I'd seen the faceless demon wield, he knocked the four of us to the ground. "John White. I will destroy your family. Thank you for being so weak."

I would have responded but I was overpowered. I knew I needed to resist the negative energy, but it was almost more than I could bear.

"Bennett White. Pathetic man. Why are you even here? Did you think you could make a difference. And Taven," he paused as he spat at me, "White. Thank you for opening a door way for me to destroy you and your family. You greatly accelerated my work. Finn White. Your family is better off without you."

His attack on my brother ignited a fire in the kindling laid by his insults to Chief and uncle Bennett. I sprung at Kane and put my hands on his shoulders. Immediately drawn into the inner realms of his being, which looked like what I would imagine the interior of an ancient crypt to look like, Long black strands hung from hooks that came from a ceiling I could not see, withered and wasted. The only light in the room was the faint glow emanating from me.

"How dare you!" rumbled Kane's voice. The entire room shook. I heard a cry. A round door covered by the same dark streamers was in front of me. I went to it, although I didn't walk, I went. As I passed the threshold of the door, the blackened strands touched me and as they did, I saw wasted women and wasted. I saw generations stripped of joy, hope and potential. I saw dismantled and ineffective families. These were families like mine only they had fallen to this devil. Kane was not bluffing. He could do what he was threatening to do. I heard another cry from the other side of this door. I passed through, haunted by the sea of tormented faces.

In the middle of the room was a little girl. She turned to me. It was the same girl I saw so long ago. The little girl who warned me not to believe anything Fiona said. The little girl who had been holding Finn's hand. "I knew you'd come to help me."

"Who are you?" I asked.

"I'm Fiona."

"How can you... I mean... Fiona's destroying my..." I stammered.

"She and I are one but Kane's done his best to divide us. I'm a shadow of her but I am who she really is." She raised her foot. It was bolted to the floor with a chain. "Can you release me? Kane will always have power over me as long as this link exists. He's enslaved me."

"Did he destroy your family too?" I asked.

"No. Like you, I would not give him what he wanted but unlike you I agreed to help him get someone else. When I did that, he bound me." She tugged at the chain. "Don't get me wrong, I never intended to actually get someone else, to get you, but I didn't realize what his hold on me would do. It was like he was always inside me, haunting me. I know I've used you. But if you don't help me, no one will. Please."

This innocent face was by itself almost enough to persuade me to cut the chains. But I wasn't sure this wasn't another trick. Fiona could be using me again somehow. But that thought didn't sit right. I knew helping her was the right thing to do. Tin clips came to mind. I focused on them and they were in my hand. I walked to her and cut the chain.

"Thank you, Taven. I will love you forever." She stood as if she was going to embrace me and vanished before she could.

The sound of raging fire filled the space. An azure flame surged into the room where I was. Before it reached me, I focused back on the prison and was transported from the place.

Murmuring now filled the hall. Some amongst the hordes that had so recently attacked us looked like they were waking up as life flickered in their countenances. Kane stared at me, his eyes betrayed his surprise. "It doesn't matter that you freed her. You and these will now join her."

In that instant, Eve's bedroom drew itself in my mind. "Hold on to me," I shouted. Chief, Uncle Bennett and Finn touched me as

I focused on the room. Kane's menacing cry faded into nothingness as we left the place.

Entering the war zone

The pink frilly comforter pulled tightly over the bed, children's books alphabetically arranged on the shelves, cartoon-like fluffy stuffed bears, pigs and dogs pointed adoringly at the little girl's head sleeping on the pillow. This was the opposite of the place we'd just been.

"You just kicked Kane's butt! Did you see him? When you went inside him he was scratching at his head like he had lice. It was so awesome. I bet he peed his pants he was so scared." Finn was acting like his favorite sports team had won the championship.

Uncle Bennett put his hand on my shoulder. "My boy, you just did the impossible. I don't know what the consequences will be but I will follow you wherever you lead."

"How long was I trapped in there?" I asked. It had seemed short, but I could have been in that prison for months.. If it wasn't for the fact that Eve looked no different than she did before, I would have thought it had been years.

Chief spoke. "I reckon it's the same day you left. Kane exists in a place between death and life. Torment, and not time, rules there. Your experience didn't require time for its intensity. We were there for hours at most, and more likely minutes."

Eve cried out in her sleep. "Finn, I thought she would be okay now?"

"I thought so too," said Finn. "You ready for another adventure?"

"Maybe with the four of us, we can finish this for good." I turned to Chief and Uncle Bennett. "Are you in?"

"You mean to go into this innocent girl's dreams? I'm not sure... I..." Chief paused. "If Finn and Bennett trust you, I do too. Count me in."

Uncle Bennett winked. I walked to the head of the bed and placed my hands on Eve's head. Finn motioned for Uncle Bennett and Chief to place their hands on my shoulders.

I wondered how Chief and Uncle Bennett were going to respond when Eve begged us to leave. Out of the darkness, Eve's voice rang out, "It's about time you guys got here. We thought you'd never come."

Relieved as I was, I was confused by what Eve meant by we.

We fell from the sky through a volley of arrows and cannon balls. Green flashes of light streaked past us. Explosions blasted exclusively on one side of the field. That could only mean Eve was being bombarded. "Follow me," I yelled as I hit the ground.

Finn, in full camouflage, was already in front of me running toward the explosions. Clods of dirt sprung up from the ground like fireworks.

Chief and Bennett cruised past us in an open-roof army jeep. A bullet grazed Uncle Bennett as they drove past. "Argh!"

A medic's pack was instantly on my back and a motorcycle between my legs. I raced after them. My front tire matched their back bumper as the jeep flew into the air in response to the explosion in front of it. Chief and Uncle Bennett were thrown into the air and on to the ground. The jeep smoldered where it sat motionless. Uncle Bennett stood on his own, so I rushed to Chief. He lay on his back on the ground. His eyes were glassy.

"They got me, my boy," he whispered.

"I've brought medicine. You're going to be fine," I said. I was pretty sure he couldn't die again, but he sure looked like he was about to. He did look like he was pretty old. Maybe we die again and this was what was going to do it for him.

Chief's eyes fluttered. If it wasn't for how weak he looked, I could have sworn he was de-aging. "I had it all wrong. You've got a great name. Taven. It sounds good to say it. An excellent name for our family."

I looked him from head to toe. I didn't see any wounds. Maybe his back was broken. I popped the lid off of a painkiller. "Hang in there. Where are you injured?"

"It's too late, too late for me. You, I want you to take the lead of the family... I have one thing I need to tell you. I... You are..." His head fell to the ground.

"Grandpa! Chief! Don't die! You can't die this way." How could we have come all this way only to lose someone at this point? When we were so close to victory.

"Taven," whispered Chief, "Got you." He now looked no older than I did.

"What do you mean... how did you?"

"I've always wanted to do that. You know, dying on the battlefield, last words. It was like the real thing, except the dying part. I can see how someone might want to spend time in a dream. I'm having a hum dinger of a time. I haven't felt this alive for a long time." He sprung to his feet and ran in the same direction Uncle Bennett and Finn had run. Over his shoulder he yelled, "By the way, I was also kidding about you being in charge. Not quite ready to give that up yet."

I ran after them. Amidst the explosions, a bunker surrounded by palm trees rose into view. Every kind of airborne implement designed to wound, maim and kill a person flew by me. It was a wonder I wasn't hit. Finn was nearly to the bunker. He leapt back and forth dodging the pockmarks left by the shower of devastation. As he opened the door, the explosions stopped. I turned around to identify the cause. A massive armor-plated vehicle appeared on the horizon. The width of one of its wheels extended the entire length of the jeep as it crushed it. Light glinted in the windshield. Turrets mounted at the front were targeted on the bunker.

"Hurry up!" yelled Finn. He held the door for Uncle Bennett who charged past him. I caught up to Chief. The rumble of the wheels shook the earth beneath us. I could feel the wind from the spinning treads on my back. We jumped for the door, and Finn closed it as the machine skidded to a stop and struck the side of the bunker, shaking the entire structure. Dust from the ceiling floated in the dimly lit room.

Chief was the first to break the silence. "This is the most fun I've had in... in... death."

"I know. Watch this." Uncle Bennett took a deep breath and exhaled. The air tickled the tips of his mustache. "I'm breathing. Hah!"

"You should have seen the last time…"

I stopped Finn. "I know you are all excited, but Fiona, Ben and Dan are outside with a gigantic truck and are about to try to make us dead. We are not here for fun. We are here to rescue Eve."

"But…" Finn stopped himself. "… fine. So where is she?"

A huge indent in the wall of the bunker punctuated a deafening blast. "They're coming."

"They're below us." Chief had a radar-looking device in hand. "Look. Under your feet. There's a hatch."

Crowbar in hand, Uncle Bennett pried the trap door open. "Are you alright down there?"

Another blast shook the bunker. "I'm going." I didn't wait. I dropped down the hole. I should have checked to see how deep it was because I fell for a long time. When I landed, I found myself at the bottom of a steel well. "Nobody's down here."

Uncle Bennett landed next to me. "What?"

"Don't come down…" I yelled as Chief came down. "Finn. Stay up there, there's no way…"

Finn slid gracefully down, his feet on opposite walls. "I made it. You should have seen you guys fall."

"We are trapped. There's no way…" I didn't get to finish. Chief had found the sweet spot in the wall, or rather the lever. He pulled it and a secret passage was revealed.

"Sorry. What was that, Taven?" asked Uncle Bennett.

"Never mind." I said as my three companions filed past me. I wondered how it was that I could go from hero to zero so quickly. There was another crash. Debris fell down the hole as I slipped into the corridor. It was dark, damp and musty. Unpleasant to say the least. I could see a light ahead.

Finn was the first to step out of the tunnel and into light. Uncle Bennett followed and said. "Well. This is unexpected."

I hurried past Chief. I pushed past Finn and Uncle Bennett. The portal opened into a room large enough to fit a hundred or so people. The floor and walls were made of stone. The room was oval in shape. The ceiling peaked to a small, central hole from which the space was lit. Backed against the wall were two people. I quickly realized the two people were Ben and Dan. "What have you done with Eve?"

"What have we done with her?" yelled Dan. "You tricked us. And you're going to pay for it."

Ben grew until his head nearly touched the lowest part of the peaked ceiling. His skin took on the appearance of leather. His nails yellowed and became thick. He picked up a rock from the ground and crushed it in his hand. "You're going down with us. Then we're taking you to Kane. He'll put you…"

"I'll have you know," Uncle Bennett cut in, "we've had a nice visit with Kane and Taven did a nice job of putting him in his place. We'll not be going back, unless we choose to go back."

Disbelief was etched on Ben's face. "Him? This guy is… I don't even know how to describe how useless he is."

Ben didn't have time to flinch before Finn had launched a stone from the sling in his hand. The giant slumped to the ground. Finn leapt on his chest. "You better watch the way you talk about my brother. Okay Dan, you're next."

Dan scanned the room then launched himself for the hole in the ceiling. Uncle Bennett snagged him with a grappling claw and pulled him to the ground. He and Chief secured him. "Where is she?"

"We don't have her," Dan whined. "When we got into the dream, Fiona left us. Told us she was going to find the girl. When she left then we were under such heavy fire the only thing for us to do was to hide in here. We ended up trapped."

"You cheated us," said Ben, who despite his immense size was easily pinned by Finn.

"And how did we do that?" I asked.

"You pretended you were weak. There's no way you should have been able to help this girl. No way you should have been able to escape from Kane. No way you should have been able to beat us. You're more than you seem. You lied to us and you tricked us... and you're going to pay for it." Ben smiled as he looked at the door. "Right about now."

Fiona had entered. She stood with a rifle in hand. She pointed it at me. "This man," she said, "did not cheat you. I did. And if you want anyone to pay for it. It should be me. I helped him escape from Kane."

"Traitor," yelled Ben.

"To who?" Fiona yelled back. "To that monster? To you? Even if I could be called a traitor, I'll happily betray the likes of you. There is one thing you should know about Taven. He rescued me. I didn't betray Kane because I didn't fight against him until after he no longer had control over me."

Eve walked into the room. "That was so much fun! Oh, it's the guy who always gets beat up in my dreams. Hi. Look what I did with my new best friend Fiona. She says she's not going to bother me anymore but she can come hang out with me anytime."

"It's time for us to go," Chief said. He, Uncle Bennett and Dan disappeared.

"Where'd they go?" asked Eve.

"Back to where they're from," said Finn as he and Ben vanished.

Eve came over to me. "You're not going to go yet, are you?"

I looked into the young girl's face. Even if this was the girl of my dreams, she wasn't now and wouldn't be for a long time. It wasn't meant to be. "It's time for us to leave." I held my hand out to Fiona. She walked over and took it without hesitation. There was no electricity. The only thing I felt from her was gratitude. "Goodbye, Eve."

The dream faded and we stood in the now crowded bedroom. Ben was held by Finn and Dan by Chief. Little Eve smiled in her sleep.

"You can't hold us forever and when you let go we're going to terrorize this little girl and everyone else in your family," menaced Ben.

"You telling lies to yourself now?" asked Finn. "We all know that this little girl kicked your butt and she'll do it again if you try to bother her."

"It's time to cut them from the family. Come to the front lawn ," said Chief.

Instantly the seven of us stood on the neatly tended lawn. I approached Dan.

"Let me go, now!" Dan shouted.

"Ignore him and do what you need to do," uncle Bennett said.

Placing my hands on his shoulders, I was drawn into his mind. Similar to Kane, hooks hung from the unseen ceiling of the crypt that housed his soul. There was one strand. It was vibrant and richly colored. I recognized the faces. I saw mine, I saw Eve's, Finn's, my mother's and my father's, my sister's and many other members of my family. I gently lifted the strand off the hook.

"They're mine. You gave them to me. You tricked me. You seduced me. You can't take them," he wailed in my mind.

"Yes, I can." The list, fully removed from the hook, vanished.

"I still know who you are," he shouted at me. "Let me go."

"Not until I've made sure there's no one else you're torturing."

"Let me be. I've got nothing to look forward to. I've never lived. I'm always dead. All is death to me. Don't torment me further. My existence is torment. Leave me be."

I ignored the wails of the pathetic soul and searched the area. I found no other strands and no other persons although there was a chain similar to the one Kane had used on Fiona but it had no occupant. "It's not too late, you know…"

"I know enough to lead Kane to you. I will get you. Save your pity for someone who needs it."

There being nothing else I could think of, I exited and felt an automatic sense of relief, like a fog had lifted.

Chief released him. He was instantly gone.

Ben struggled as I approached him. "You'll regret this. Let me be." Uncle Bennett helped Finn restrain him.

"I would regret not doing this more," I said, placing my hands on his shoulders.

His voice rang in my mind. "You can't see this. No. Get out."

I entered his mind. Although dark and dangerous, the setting wasn't so crypt-like, so final. It seemed like I was in a bear's cave. Several hooks hung from the ceiling. I quickly found my family strand and removed it. "Good riddance. Your disgusting family was sullying my being. Weak. Loathsome. Pathetic. Take it and have it."

Like Dan, the other hooks were empty but one other strand grew right out of the wall. This list was lined with faces I did not recognize, except for one near the bottom, which was faded and charred. "Janice?"

"Get out. Take your names, but stop looking at mine. It's none of your business. Let me be."

"This isn't your family, Ben. You are going to give me this. You aren't going to torment anyone anymore." I attempted to remove the list but could not remove it from the wall. Nothing came to mind that would assist me.

"This is... this is... my family. Leave me alone." His voice was broken. I relaxed for a moment and was thrown from his consciousness like a bull rider from a bull. As I landed, Ben struggled free from the grasp of Uncle Bennett and Finn and disappeared.

"I guess it's my turn," said Fiona. "I won't struggle. I don't want to hurt you. I really want you to have your family back."

After everything I'd been through with Fiona, I didn't want to see her go now. This couldn't all be coincidence. "You could stay in our family."

Finn looked apprehensive. Fiona glanced at him and then back to me. "It's time, Taven. If I come into the family, it will be the right way."

As I walked to her to put my hands on her shoulders, I wondered what she meant when she said she'd come into the family by the right way. I entered her consciousness. The space was bright and light. There were no hooks. a single streamer lined with unfamiliar faces danced across the room. Little Fiona stood before me. "Thank you for helping me, Taven. This is my family. This is the reason I used you. I'm so sorry but once I met you I knew you could help me and save me. I'm really sorry for all those mean things I did. I had to. To protect them and to protect you. I always tried not to go further than I needed to.

Fiona walked to me with my strand in her hands. "Here's your family, they are amazing. Especially, Finn."

I now understood why Finn looked apprehensive and why he was always defending her. They were a match. They were a pair. I tried really hard not to feel jealous that my brother had found his match when mine was seemingly forever out of reach. "Just one question. Why did you say you will always love me?"

"Because I will. You made it possible for me to be who I really am and helped me find Finn in the process. If he'll have me, and I think he will, then we'll have a long time together and I'll love you for every minute of it."

"I guess we will, sister." I hugged the little girl and left the solitude of the place.

Not alone anymore

Soon after I had exited Fiona's consciousness, Fiona and Finn, hand-in-hand had gone off somewhere together. It's almost like they planned it this way. I was left alone with Uncle Bennett and Chief.

"Let's get out of here," the much younger Chief suggested. I didn't object. Chief, Bennett and I huddled and were in an instant in my clearing, with trees surrounding us, an ever-flowing river near. The younger version of Chief seemed so much more at ease.

Chief patted me on the shoulder. "We needed you to do this without remembering, without seeing. Believe it or not it was hard for me, for us, to watch you do this. You've got a gift, Taven, that's born of your past but you needed to find it independent of your past."

I was overwhelmed by this visual and emotional change in Chief. But I didn't feel strong. Finn was strong. Fiona was strong. "What strength do I have?"

"No one and I mean no one has kept themselves after being in a dream. Not only have you kept yourself but you kept others. You made a path for Finn, Bennett and I to follow. You rescued an innocent little girl and in the process you did the impossible. You made a way for the redemption of a dream junkie."

"What about Ben and..."

"Fiona chose to follow the way you prepared. Just because the others didn't doesn't diminish your strength. You opened the door for the release of a person from Kane's enslavement."

An unspeakable assurance confirmed what Chief said. I guess I'd never considered something as small as my will, as my choice to be so important, to be strength. All I wanted now was to use that strength to help others. "Ben had his own family... I saw Janice's face on that list."

"Janice?" Uncle Bennett asked.

"Janice. The one who's father entered the dream to help with her self-confidence. She belongs to Ben's family list." I said. "We've got to stop him. You seem to know that family. Let's go see them and help them get Ben carved out. I would have done it but I couldn't. Maybe it wasn't the father that harmed Janice after all. Maybe it was Ben..."

"Hold on there, Taven," said Uncle Bennett.

"What do you mean hold on? What's more important than saving another family from these demons? I've found my purpose."

Chief laughed. "Will you play a role in rescuing Janice and her generations? There's a strong possibility. But first things must come first. There's a lady you know who's looking forward to seeing you." When I turned to look, Chief vanished, his laughter the only thing remaining.

Uncle Bennett saluted me and said, "Great job." And then he was gone.

That's when I noticed the person standing on the other edge of the field, too far to be recognized.

I walked towards this person, who wore a long hooded cloak that was so long the bottom folded several times on the ground. "Who are you?"

As soon as I called, the person turned toward the path that led downtown and walked. The cloak must have split in the middle, otherwise the person would have tripped on the extensive fabric that fanned behind her like the train of a wedding gown. The hood fell back revealing long mahogany colored hair. I hastened my pace to catch up to her, but she was far enough ahead that I didn't immediately catch her. I would have drawn my way to her, but somehow it didn't seem right to pursue in any way other than by foot. She veered towards the river, behind the line of trees, the same place Finn and I had skipped stones. Maybe this was Auntie Sophie with a message. Something to do with completing my task, with fulfilling my purpose.

I turned the corner and was surprised to find a woman dressed in a hoodie and blue jeans. Her back was to me. The cloak was heaped on the ground behind her. "Who are you?"

"I'm not your auntie," the woman said as she turned towards me.

Was I seeing things? Eve was standing in front of me, looking like she did that day at the hot dog cart. *Should I hug her? Should I kiss her? No that's too far, I couldn't even remember if we ever went on a date. No, this was too good to be true. The real Eve was in danger and this was intended to delay me. This was Kane's trick.*

"Don't you recognize me?" she asked in a perfectly familiar tone.

"You look a lot like a girl I used to know," I said, leaving a slight edge to my voice.

"Used to know? What happened? Did you forget me?" she asked, unmoved by my gruffness.

I walked closer to her, familiarity nearly overwhelming me. "There's a ten year old girl that's really you. I know what you're up to."

"Do I look like a ten year-old girl to you?" she asked, her amusement palpable.

My resistance to her failing quickly, I stepped backwards, hoping to make the path before I succumbed to her. "You're trying to trick me. You're trying to keep me from my purpose, from my destiny."

For the first time, she started towards me, and as she did, my heart leapt in spite of myself. "I'm not trying to keep you from your destiny. I am your destiny. It's me," she took my hands in hers, "it's Eve."

The instant her hand met mine all doubt fled. She smiled and leaned into me. Her lips touched mine, it was as though mine were made for hers and hers for mine. Like a projector at long last unjammed, my movie began to play.

Summer had ended and we both were off to university. Both to the same school. Eve zigzagged up the hallway, greeting nearly everyone, stopping for a quick chat here and there. I stood at my locker, half hidden by its door, half watching her approach. We'd had our moment at the hot dog cart, but it seemed too good to be true, so trembling I waited to see if she'd come say "hi" to me. It was agony watching her stop and go, talk and flash that smile of hers, wondering if I really was any more special to her than any of the other people she interacted with. Worrying backed me into a defensive position, yesterday was a dream and dreams never last. I stopped watching her and fumbled around with the binders stacked at the top of my locker.

"Taven, how are you?" she beamed.

Startled, I grabbed the top binder and smacked her on the head.

"Ow," she said, rubbing her head.

I had no idea why I had done that or what I was now supposed to do. "Hey… so… umm… do you want to go to a movie?"

Still rubbing her head and eyeing me suspiciously, she said, "Will you hit me again if I don't?"

"I am so sorry I don't know what…"

"Neither do I, but as long as you don't knock me in the head with anything else, it's a date."

It was during the second inning of her brother's fall classic baseball game that I held her hand for the first time. She snuck away while he was on the bench. I tried to get my cart out as often as possible on weekends to earn as much money as I could for the upcoming week at college. We talked for a bit and as I cleaned the surface of my cart, she put her hand near mine and I grabbed it.

Not much later I stood with her on the sidewalk in front of her parent's home after a fun night with her and with friends. I wanted to kiss her but I couldn't muster the courage. I walked her right up to the gate. She hugged me and opened the gate She walked through but at the last possible moment I grabbed her hand and pulled her to me. We kissed.

I took her to the park where I learned about Finn's accident, the park where I began my adventure in the afterlife. She looked at me and said, without a hint of doubt, "You'll see him again."

Time passed by and I was on my knee asking her to marry me, promising her forever.

I saw myself carrying her into our first little apartment.

I cringed over the first argument to interrupt our marital bliss; it had something to do with the toothpaste tube.

I struggled to restrain my emotion when I recognized the baby bump, didn't resist any more when I saw the birth of Tim, our little boy. Then came Nancy, then Gavin and finally Jane.

Hand in hand we travelled along as five years, ten years, twenty years passed. Grand babies came.

My parents passed away.

Great grand babies came.

My sister, Karen, passed away.

Not long after I sat beside a bed, my sweetheart lying near death. Her body bore the marks of a long and full life, but her eyes shone like the first time I met her. I kissed her. She whispered that she loved me. Hand in hand, I watched her eyes close never to open again. But before she died, she said, without a hint of doubt, "We'll be together again."

Lonely years followed. No one could fill the void she left. I struggled with the doubt that I wouldn't see her again.

A great great grand baby was born. Her name was Eve. The same one I helped and came to in her dreams.

I saw myself, a short time later, surrounded by children, children's children and children's children's children me the one now lying, knowing death was soon to take me. Little Eve, now ten years old, wept uncontrollably and oh, how I loved her, she was my Eve's namesake and so much like her in every way. I placed my trembling hand on her cheek and said, "We'll see each other again someday."

My body tired, old and worn, my heart filled with satisfaction, with posterity around me, I closed my eyes.

These and millions of additional drops of experience filled the reservoirs of my memory. I opened my eyes. My dream girl stood before my eyes. She had chosen to be with me. "Eve."

"I told you we'd see each other again," she said, the sound better than a symphony or a baby's first cry.

Pure joy filled me as I held my Eve close.

I am Taven.

ABOUT THE AUTHOR

Mike Jackson lives in Alberta, Canada with his wife Natasha and their five children. Both he and Natasha grew up in families with more than the per capita average of kids. He is a lawyer by day, an aspiring author by night and always a husband and father.

More Books by Mike Jackson

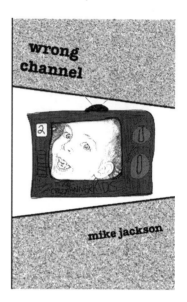

www.mdjackson.com

Got Kid? Got iPhone? Get Thandros!

Wanna try Tic Tac Toe with Thandros for free?

How about a free maze quest with Oliver?

Don't know how to read these?

All you need is your iPhone and a QR Reader, available on the

iTunes app store.

www.thandrosmedia.com

Made in the USA
Charleston, SC
02 December 2012